All's Fair in Loat and War

Baker's Rise Mysteries

Book Six

R. A. Hutchins

For the bird lovers, the fruit farmers and
the secret seed stashers,
Reggie thanks you all!

CONTENTS

If you follow this list in order, you will have made a perfect
Orange and Apricot Loaf Cake *to enjoy whilst you read!*

ONE

Flora stretched out her legs underneath her new rustic kitchen table and took a sip of Earl Grey – almost straight out of the teapot, it was still too hot, but she was parched so suffered through the heat on her tongue. Reggie watched intently from his perch on the back of the chair next to her, tilting his head to one side and clucking quietly.

"Good bird," Flora whispered, setting her mug back down and reaching out to stroke his soft feathers. The afternoon summer sun shone low through the wide kitchen window, making his greens and yellows glow and reminding Flora of the tropical origins of his species.

"My Flora, my Flora all shook up!" Reggie squawked

happily, repeating one of his newly acquired phrases. Unfortunately for Flora, the company who she had hired to lay carpets in the upstairs bedrooms and the new parquet floor in what had been the dingy dining room – and was now to be a beautiful drawing room that could serve as a function room for events – seemed to only employ fitters who were superfans of the late Elvis Presley. Despite her trying to encourage Reggie to stay in the study, the sociable parrot had insisted on perching where the action was.

"Just 'My Flora' will do," Flora tried to correct him, knowing it was like banging her head against a brick wall. Unfortunately, her own tastes in music didn't extend to 1960s rock n roll. Nor country music or gospel for that matter. This grumpy response didn't seem to inhibit her feathered friend, though.

"Can't help... falling in love... with you!" Reggie continued, apparently oblivious to how much it annoyed his owner, though the way he studiously avoided eye contact led Flora to believe the little parrot knew exactly what her thoughts were!

Thankfully, the floor was on track to be finished today and with it the last of the workmen would leave the manor house after what had been months of disruption and a small fortune from Flora's savings account. She pushed that thought aside, the worry that niggled away at her in the rare quiet times like this one – that she had spent so much on renovating The Rise, that she had little left for its upkeep. Even with the rents, the tearoom and bookshop incomes, potential money from functions held at the manor house as well as Harry's wise accounting advice, Flora worried that she was going to struggle to maintain the place.

It had been worth it though, Flora kept telling herself that – the whole house was classy and elegant and, she hoped, brought back to its former glory – she just wished it could have cost slightly less, in both financial and emotional terms. The stress of overseeing everything had certainly taken its toll, and in her private moments, Flora wondered whether it had all been worth it. Would she ever feel at home in this place the way she did in the coach house, for example? Even any affection for the old pile of bricks would be an improvement.

Flora shook her head as she took another sip of her tea, trying to free her mind of the worrisome thoughts. She had so much to look forward to. Adam was meeting her here in the next hour to go over some details with their wedding planners, and then she had the vintage clothing Try and Buy sale tonight, here at the manor house, which Tanya had helped her organise. The

clothes were one of the few types of items still left over
from the house clearance, and Flora presumed they
had once belonged to Harold Baker's mother and
grandmother. A lot of furniture and artwork had gone
to auction, and raised a decent sum which had
immediately been swallowed up in the decorating
costs. Flora had kept her favourite antique pieces of
furniture, some paintings, nearly all the china crockery
and silverware, and two old jewellery boxes which, at
first glance, were full of costume pieces. She and Tanya
had left the boxes out with the rails of clothes, in case
any of their village friends wished to accessorise their
new-to-them outfits.

Even those villagers of the older generation, who
maybe had no intention of buying a pair of genuine 70s
flares, were coming. Flora frowned slightly, then
caught herself and tried to smooth out her forehead –
she certainly didn't want to age any faster than she
already was, and heaven forbid she bring on any more
of the awful hot flushes she'd been having lately – but
the thought of Betty didn't bring the usual warm glow
of friendship and belonging that Flora normally
experienced. It hadn't done so, in fact, since she had
told the older woman that they were hiring a wedding
company to plan and cater the event, complete with
decorations, cake, the whole kit and caboodle. To say

Betty had been disappointed would be an understatement. Indeed, her friend had been very vocal on how Flora had let the village down by not letting the ladies of the local W.I. help her with the organising and baking.

What seemed to peeve Betty most was the fact that Flora hadn't asked her to bake the wedding cake. Flora had good reasons – mainly that Betty was already busy with Harry, but also that she would have insisted on the traditional rich fruit cake. Adam has suggested that they have something less formal, less traditional, and Flora had agreed. Together they had decided to have different types of loaf cake, balanced in a modern-looking structure – not as sweet and something for everyone. Betty had poo-pooed the idea and not even tried to hide the fact that her nose had been pushed sorely out of joint.

This was just one of a number of things that had made Flora more and more inclined to share Adam's view that they should have a quieter, scaled-down event. Not that they had really had any choice in the matter, however. Being the lady of the manor, so to speak, made this nigh on impossible, because to leave out even one family from the village would have been seen as an insult. So, Flora had had no choice but to go all-in, and a marquee had been hired for the back lawn, as well as a live band for the new function room. With only three and a half weeks to go, Flora should be feeling excited. And she was. Really.

"Strangers! Strangers with money! Let's rock!" Reggie screeched, flapping his wings, as there was a soft tap on the back door and the gardener, Laurie, poked his head around.

"Sorry Reggie, no money, but I do have a banana!" Laurie laughed, producing the fruit from his lunch box, which he set on the counter as he looked in the cutlery drawer for a knife.

After her last experience with hiring someone to work on the estate grounds, Flora would have understandably been very nervous treading the same path again had she not been introduced to Lawrence by his godmother, Lily. Flora had offered lodging to him, his lovely wife Rosa, and their toddler son Matias here at the big house, but they had chosen instead to live in the village, renting the small building owned by the estate which last year had briefly been set to be a candy store. They had moved into the apartment above, and Rosa was planning to open a craft shop there. She had learnt to embroider and crochet from her Spanish grandmother and had already impressed the village ladies at the Knit and Natter group with her skills. Her shop was going to sell yarns, threads, buttons, fabric... all the things which made the village ladies clap for joy! She often brought Laurie's lunch up the hill for him, and little Matias would play in the gardens, encouraging even Flora to the occasional game of hide and seek.

"How are you getting on with the ornamental gardens?" Flora asked, knowing that her gardener was putting himself under pressure to have everything perfect by her wedding day.

"They're coming along nicely," he smiled, and Flora immediately felt calmer. Laurie had that effect on everyone, such a gentle, kind man, his blue eyes were always smiling even when he was stressed. Other than when he had been re-introduced to her former gardener, Mitch, the biological father of Matias, Flora had never heard the man so much as raise his voice. The family were a lovely addition to the village, to be sure.

"Perfect, you've done such a grand job with the rose garden, Billy would be proud," Flora had told Laurie all about the man who had tended the estate gardens for decades, and had shared with him the photographs that had been found during the house clearance.

"Thank you so much for saying that, Flora," Laurie

blushed as he looked out of the window, "I'm going to call it a day, but I'll be back bright and early in the morning."

"Of course, tell Rosa I'm looking forward to seeing her tonight at the clothes sale."

"Will do!" He laid the chopped banana on the table for Reggie, who sang, "You give me strength to carry on…" in gratitude.

"Silly bird!" Flora chided.

"You silly old bird!" Reggie squawked and Flora smiled as she heard Laurie's chuckle as he left.

TWO

The clatter of boots in the hallway signalled to Flora that the floor fitters had completed their job and a moment later the four men appeared in the kitchen.

"Hide it all!" Reggie shrieked, even though he had become more used to the workmen coming and going recently.

"Hush!" Flora whispered.

"We're all done, Mrs. Miller, it's looking grand even if I do say so myself," Jeff, the foreman, reached out to shake Flora's hand.

"That's brilliant, thank you, I'll take a good look when my fiancé gets here," Flora smiled as the men filed out.

"Oh, er thank you for the book recommendation," the

small, wiry man in front of her hovered uncomfortably, waiting to speak until his colleagues had left, "that Wilbur Smith was just the ticket."

Over the course of the fortnight that the team had been working at the manor house, Flora had had a few conversations with Vic, who had rather embarrassedly expressed his love of reading when she had mentioned that she owned the Bookshop on The Rise, "You're very welcome. If you're ever over this way, do pop into the bookshop, I have a few more of his books in the library corner to borrow."

"Will do, will do," he blushed and rushed out to join the others in the van.

"Good riddance!" Reggie shrieked in his wake.

"Reginald parrot, what has come over you?" Flora asked softly, nuzzling the little bird in the crook of her neck. Though, to be fair, she herself breathed a sigh of relief knowing that they were the last of the contractors to finish in the house, for the next while at least.

Flora had just finished making a cafetiere of coffee for Adam and the wedding planners to share, and a large pot of Earl Grey in case they fancied having a cup of tea like her, when the man himself arrived. Flora swallowed the words on the tip of her tongue that wanted to comment on her fiancé being early for once, when he himself made the joke for her.

"I bet you weren't expecting to see me so soon," Adam flashed her a grin and kissed Flora gently on the lips.

"Well, I wasn't going to say anything but… it is a pleasant surprise, yes!" Flora thought briefly of the other meetings they'd had to discuss the wedding with the Crawford family who were doing all the organising, and recalled three that she had attended alone due to her fiancé's last-minute need to cancel their plans, and two others where Adam had been at least half an hour late as he'd again been caught up at work. Flora understood though, his job as a detective certainly wasn't your usual nine to five!

"It was quiet in the station, so I finished my paperwork and headed out. As long as there are no murders in the area over the next few hours, I'm all yours!"

"I like the sound of that," Flora added Adam's usual three sugars and some milk to his coffee cup and stirred absentmindedly, enjoying the new peace and quiet in the house as Adam went to take off his coat and tie.

"So, what's the news?" Adam asked, coming back into the kitchen, and unable to help another quick peck on the cheek.

Flora appreciated his sweet affection and took his hand in hers, "Well, the floor fitters just finished, so we can go and take a quick look if you like, and then the Crawfords should be here in ten minutes or so. If they don't start one of their usual arguments, the meeting should only last about an hour."

"I've never known a family to bicker so much – in a professional, public setting, I mean," Adam added stiffly. A shadow crossed his face, and not for the first time Flora wondered about Adam's own family. That was one subject on which he had always been a closed book, and Flora did not press him on it. He had told her that he'd been married to his job in the police force since his early twenties, having never wanted to do anything else, but hadn't elaborated on his motivations for this. Flora had wondered, of course, but was content that he would share with her in due course, as their relationship evolved naturally.

"I know! You'd think that you wouldn't work together if there was that much disagreement! Lizzie recommended them to me, as she's friendly with Sylvia the mum. I think the business was Sylvia's originally, then from what I understand David was made redundant and joined her to help with the subcontracting for marquees and such like. Then Tammy joined the family business after a particularly bad break up. I don't know the details, that was as much as Lizzie told me. Apparently, sometimes people want their pets included in the wedding ceremony, so she's asked along to capture some portraits and that's how she met them."

"You aren't getting any ideas about having Reggie involved in our vows are you?" Adam asked, and Flora could tell that he was only half joking.

"Ha! Well, maybe a feathery ringbearer…"

"Well, I… ah…"

"I'm only joking," Flora squeezed Adam's hand and stood to stretch, "can you imagine him in the spotlight? He'd never be happy to fade into the background again!"

They laughed then, just as there was a sharp rap on the back door. It didn't sound like the rather loud discussions that usually heralded the arrival of the Crawfords, and Adam quickly stood to answer the door, his senses alert.

"Blackett!" Flora heard Adam greet his colleague and work partner, the surprise in his voice evident, "Come in, what brings you out this way?"

"There's been a development, Bramble, and I need to speak with you... matter of urgency, I'm afraid... apologies for the intrusion, Mrs. Miller."

"Not at all, Detective Blackett," Flora did find it slightly odd that even off duty both men always referred to each other by their surnames, and when she thought on it, she realised she didn't even know Blackett's first name. Not that her interactions with him had been in any way social. She knew that Adam held him in very high regard, and had worked with the man for over a decade, but Flora was also aware that the detective had not initially approved of her relationship with Adam, given that it had developed following the murder investigation into her predecessor, Harold Baker. She hoped that he was rather less disapproving of the situation now though – not that they needed Blackett's approval, but since Adam had asked his friend to be his best man, Flora hoped she could get to know him a little better at least. Her fiancé's choice didn't come as much of a shock, as Flora had never heard Adam mention any friends other than the people he worked with, yet she had worried slightly how Blackett's infamously dour expression would fit in with what she hoped would be a happy wedding party.

"Thank you, I... ah..."

This was the first time that Flora had ever seen the man lost for words, and looking closely she saw the tremble in his hands and sheen of sweat on his paler-than-usual brow, "Would you like to sit down, detective? There's fresh coffee here... or tea?"

Flora noticed the pointed look that Blackett gave Bramble and got the distinct impression that what he had to say needed some privacy, "I was just going through to the front room to look out for the wedding planners, come on Reggie!"

The little bird had already shrieked "Not that jerk!" three times on quick repeat, and Flora decided it would be a good idea to remove him from the room anyway.

She assumed that, although it was the first time he had ever appeared unannounced when not investigating a case in which Flora was involved, Blackett's visit was work-related and Flora didn't give it any further thought as she and Reggie made their way to the front of the manor house.

THREE

"I'm telling you, Sylvia, a horse-drawn carriage would have been a great addition!"

"Yes, but Flora and Adam want to walk up from the church together, with their guests."

"Those horses always smell, anyway, Dad!"

Flora could hear the family debating the subject of her arrival from the church to The Rise, not for the first time, and let out a small sigh of exasperation as she opened the heavy front door to catch them as they made their way around to the usual back entrance.

"Hello! How are we all?" Flora spoke loudly over them, as she had found that was the only way to get a quick resolution to their noise. No matter how many times she had said that she wanted a simple, classy occasion, one or other of her wedding planners was always keen to up the ante. This invariably led to a rather heated discussion in which, more often than not, Flora found herself nothing more than a silent observer and had wondered on more than one occasion why she had ever hired planners in the first place. Perhaps Betty was right and she should have kept it in the village. It was too late now though...

"Afternoon, Flora, have you had any more thoughts on the horse and carriage idea?"

"Ah well, I thought we'd taken that firmly off the table, David, there are only three weeks or so left after all. Just the finishing touches to discuss, I thought," Flora said as she led them to the sitting room, trying to inject the same firmness in her voice that she knew Tanya or Betty would have used.

"Quite right too," Sylvia agreed, giving her husband a look that dared him to mention it again, and accepting Flora's offer of a seat on one of the velvet sofas.

"And how's Reggie?" Tammy walked straight over to the bird's perch and he nuzzled happily into the palm of the woman's hand.

"Take my hand... take my whole life too..." Reggie chirped happily and the tension in the room seemed to dissolve somewhat, much to Flora's relief, as they all chuckled.

"I see Elvis still hasn't left the building," David joked.

"Hmm, unfortunately not," Flora smiled ruefully, "anyway, the drinks are on the kitchen table, so I'll just pop through and get them."

"I'll help you," Tammy offered, and the two women walked along the cheerily decorated hallway chatting comfortably about the flowers that Flora had chosen a few weeks ago and how well they would match the peach and cornflower blue colour scheme for the wedding.

"Yes, I'm confident that they'll…" Tammy stopped dead in the doorway to the kitchen as she saw Adam and Blackett still deep in quiet discussion at the kitchen table. A discussion which, to Flora, looked to be rather intense.

It took a couple of seconds for the men to notice that they were there, and when Blackett lifted his head and saw the woman with Flora, his face registered a look of pure shock. Indeed, it perfectly mirrored the expression on Tammy's face. Flora looked between the two, aware that the thick tension in the air could be cut with a metaphorical knife. Normally, Adam would have said something to defuse the ominous silence, but when Flora looked closely at her own husband-to-be she saw an anguish there that had never been present in his expression before. It immediately made her wonder what exactly Blackett had come to discuss. But that would have to wait as for now she was stuck hovering in the doorway with her guest.

"Well, ah the teapot should still be hot and Adam can quickly make us some fresh coffee," Flora said, rather too loudly, bustling into the kitchen and picking up a tray for the cups and saucers.

"Micah," Tammy whispered behind her, and it took Flora a good few seconds to realise that the woman was referring to Blackett.

The sound of a chair scraping followed, and Flora half turned so that she could watch the pair out of the corner of her eye as she busied herself with the crockery.

"Tamara," Blackett's voice was low and hoarse, his eyebrows settling into the ominous line of displeasure which Flora had come to recognise. He stood to face the woman, recognition and anger warring across his features, along with something else which Flora couldn't quite pinpoint.

Flora had the distinct feeling that she and Adam

should make themselves scarce, but her fiancé seemed oblivious to the uncomfortable scene which was unfolding, simply running his hands through his hair and looking at the tabletop as if it were the most scintillating of views.

There was nothing for it, but for Flora to take matters into her own hands, "I'm guessing you both know each other?" she asked cheerily, assuming Betty's obtusely thick skin and ability to blunder her way through social discomfort, and hoping suddenly that the pair's acquaintance hadn't come about because Tammy had been involved in a murder enquiry.

"You could say that," Blackett said without turning, still studying Tammy's face intently as tears began to stream down the woman's cheeks. As if he couldn't bear the sight of her distress, the detective moved quickly forwards until he was toe to toe with Tammy, then just as swiftly pulled her into the circle of his arms, where she appeared to melt against his chest.

"Oh! I… ah, Adam, I think they'll be waiting for us in the sitting room," Flora hastily grabbed the teapot to add to the tray and nudged Adam with her hip.

"Oh, yes," Adam replied, standing as if on autopilot, "we'll discuss that first thing tomorrow in the station, Blackett." Only then did her fiancé cast a glance towards his colleague and Flora saw his startled expression as he saw the two people still entwined in a close embrace.

"What was all that about?" Adam whispered as they shut the kitchen door firmly behind them.

"I could ask you the same," Flora replied, unable to keep the consternation from her tone.

"What? Oh, ah, Blackett just had some information about... a case," the deliberately vague answer was not lost on Flora, and had they had more time then she would have definitely pressed harder for a less flaky explanation.

As it was, Sylvia and David were deep in another rather loud 'discussion' as the couple entered the room, and Reggie was listening intently from the arm of the sofa, interjecting the occasional "Now there's trouble!" and "There'll be hell to pay!" for dramatic effect.

"Ahem," Flora cleared her throat loudly to get their attention, placing the tray on the antique mahogany coffee table and then joining Adam on the opposite settee, "if you have today's agenda handy, then let's get started, shall we?"

"Yes, of course," Sylvia gave her husband a harsh glare, in contradiction to the placatory tone she directed towards Flora, "I think there are eleven small things to discuss."

Flora swallowed her sigh at that news, but Adam was not quite so polite, "Really? Surely to goodness we must have been through every wedding-related topic known to man over the past two months. What could there possibly be left to discuss?"

Flora had rarely seen her fiancé this agitated, only really when she herself had been hurt or in danger. Her stomach began to get the sinking feeling that signalled something bad was about to happen – the gut instinct that she had learned not to ignore – and she turned to face the man she loved.

"Adam, I'm sure it'll be quick…"

Flora didn't even get her sentence finished before Adam interjected, his hair sticking out at odd angles where he continued to rake his fingers through it, "Do we really need all this pomp and circumstance Flora? Really? I told you from the beginning that I wanted a smaller, more private affair, and it's grown into this… this monster." He gesticulated wildly with his arms, causing Reggie to start swooping over them, his little senses on alert.

"Well, I..." Flora began, but he clearly wasn't finished.

"I thought that by giving ourselves just a few months to organise it, that that would limit the scope..."

"Oh, and here was me thinking it was because you wanted to become my husband as quickly as possible..." Flora tried to hide the hurt in her voice.

"I'll go and fetch Tammy, what on earth could be keeping that girl?" David stated, standing suddenly as if he couldn't bear the awkward atmosphere – something which struck Flora as odd, considering the number of times she had been forced to sit through him arguing with his own wife.

"I do, of course I do," Adam replied, though it came out as more of an exasperated bark than a reassurance.

"Perhaps we could reconvene for a more appropriate day," Sylvia began, "though we are very limited on time now..." She was cut off by the sound of loud shouting from the hallway, two male voices echoing off the high ceiling, and a woman's plaintiff cry.

"Pipe down!" Reggie screeched, flying straight to the door. Adam was already on his feet and rushing to open it with Sylvia hot on his heels, whilst Flora simply stood slowly, her head whirring and the nauseous feeling rising to her throat.

FOUR

"I warned you! I did! That if you ever came within viewing distance of my daughter again, that I wouldn't be responsible for my actions!" David was shouting, from his position pinned against the hallway wall by Adam who was trying to contain the man, as Flora approached the scene.

Sylvia was holding her daughter close, cradling Tammy's head to her shoulder, as her irate husband tried to wriggle out of Adam's grasp long enough to reach Blackett. The man in question stood in the doorway to the kitchen, his eyes mere slits, though Flora saw a blotchy puffiness to his features which was never normally present.

"I'm sure we can discuss this reasonably," Flora began

as Reggie shrieked, "Secrets and Lies!" three times on repeat, drowning out whatever else she was about to say.

It was as the small bird was about to dive bomb Blackett's head for the second time that he himself spoke, "My apologies, Tamara, I had no idea you would be here." He gave the distraught woman one fleeting look of what Flora could only describe as yearning, before turning swiftly and leaving the scene via the kitchen. The sound of the back door slamming shut permeated the sudden silence, which lasted only a brief moment before Tammy let out a loud gasp and then a sob.

"Hush, he's gone now," Sylvia whispered to her daughter, stroking her hair.

"I don't want him gone!" Tammy shrieked, standing suddenly straight and shouting at her father, "It's all your fault! It always was!"

Adam had let go of the man who was now leaning against the wall, as if all the fight had been taken out of him, "I'm sorry, Tam," he whispered, though Flora was more focused on the fact that her own fiancé had left without a word, following his colleague out of the house.

Despite the Crawford family leaving quickly after that, there was no sign of either Adam or his car when Flora went to seek him out. She tried hard to tamp down the feelings of anxiety and disappointment which his unannounced exit provoked. Admittedly, there was some anger there too, and Flora found herself sitting at the kitchen table, wringing her hands in silent contemplation for at least half an hour until the buzzing of her mobile phone brought her out of her internal dialogue.

"Somebody else!" Reggie shrieked, still thoroughly unsettled by the afternoon's events.

Hoping it would be Adam, Flora rushed to grab the source of the noise, experiencing a deep sense of disappointment when she saw Tanya's name flash up on the screen.

"Flora! So sorry, running late, on way now," Tanya's breathless voice caught Flora off guard, making her realise that it must be even later than she had thought as Tanya was coming along to help her get set up for the evening event.

"Oh, don't worry, I'm running late myself, see you soon," Flora quickly ended the call, realising she had not eaten, had not changed into one of the vintage outfits she had chosen, and had not prepared the crockery and nibbles for the ladies who were attending the clothes sale. Suddenly, none of it seemed to matter and she couldn't seem to make herself care. Flora felt numb.

"My Flora!" Reggie whispered, snuggling up against her neck, "My Flora!"

"Good bird," Flora replied gently, stroking his downy soft feathers absentmindedly.

"I am here!" Tanya announced loudly and, Flora thought, rather unnecessarily. Thankfully, she was no longer feeling the complete numbness of earlier. Unfortunately, it had been replaced by irritability and a total lack of patience.

To cover this, Flora simply smiled and accepted the quick hug which Tanya offered. Even that wasn't enough to break through Flora's shell of apathy, nor did she give her usual smile when Reggie swooped onto Tanya's head, squawking, "She's a corker!" He didn't get his usual response from Tanya either, however, and so the bird flew off in apparent disgust.

Despite always being the life and soul of the party, Tanya had an empathy and sensitivity to her which meant she immediately sensed that there was something wrong with her friend.

"Something has happened?" she asked, stepping back slightly to study Flora's features.

"No, well, not really, I mean," Flora shrugged her shoulders as she mumbled her reply, aware she wasn't convincing anyone.

"Hmm, well, we have time to talk it through. The clothes are already sorted onto the rails upstairs and the others aren't due to arrive for another half an hour at least," Tanya spoke as she filled the kettle and looked in the cupboard for two large mugs, normally used by the various workmen, "a lot of tea is needed, I think. And some of these chocolate muffins!"

They took their hot drinks into the study, which Flora had made into more of a cosy sitting room, much more comfortable than the formal reception room at the front of the house. A small desk had been placed under the window, next to Reggie's perch, and the rest of the room was dedicated to a squishy sofa and two wide, tub-shaped armchairs in mis-matching fabrics. Adorned with cushions and throws, this was the room Flora had taken to spending her time in when she didn't have guests.

"So," Tanya began, when it was obvious Flora wasn't going to take the lead in explaining what was wrong, "it has been a bad day?"

"Most of it was fine, and Adam even arrived early for out meeting with the Crawfords, but it seemed to go downhill quickly after that," Flora sighed and took a rather slow sip of her tea.

Either oblivious to, or totally disregarding her friend's stalling tactic, Tanya pressed on, "The meeting didn't go well?"

"No, you could say that," Flora decided it would be quicker to just tell Tanya what had happened and so gave a hurried explanation of Blackett's unexpected visit, of the shared moment of recognition between he and Tammy, of Adam's anger about their own wedding plans, and about the showdown in the hallway.

"And you don't know why the other detective showed up here in the first place?" Tanya asked gently.

"Nope, no idea! It was clearly something serious though, I had just assumed Adam would tell me afterwards."

"And he left without saying goodbye?"

"Exactly. If I'm honest, that's the bit which hurts the most. Totally out of character for Adam," Flora fought back the tears. *At least I don't feel numb anymore,* "I'm not sure if he left so abruptly because he's angry about the wedding, because he wanted to catch up to Blackett, or maybe even both. Either way, I feel like he's punishing me a bit for having the wedding all my own way. Even though it's turned into something I don't want either! I never really did if I'm honest. Goodness, I do sound very dramatic, don't I?" Flora gave a watery attempt at a smile.

"Do you want me to hold the fort here while you call him?" Tanya asked kindly.

"Thank you, but no, if I speak to him I think it needs to be face to face. It'll have to wait till tomorrow now," Flora struggled to speak past the lump in her throat.

"My Flora, silly old bird," Reggie flew from his perch onto Flora's arm, causing her tears to fall faster.

They sat in companionable silence for a while, with even Tanya appearing subdued. So caught up was she in her own woes, that Flora didn't give a second thought to her friend's melancholy, assuming it was her own mood that had rubbed off on the other woman.

"Come on," Flora said eventually, standing and rubbing Tanya's arm in gratitude, "let's get this show on the road."

FIVE

"I tell you, it'll look like that game the young'uns play in the pub, Wenga!"

Flora bit her tongue to stop the retort that threatened to slip out as Betty made yet another reference to the wedding cake. In truth, her upcoming nuptials were the last subject Flora wanted to discuss, and unfortunately the first thing on everyone else's mind.

"You mean Jenga, Betty," Shona corrected, smiling indulgently at the older woman.

"Aye well, either way, a wedding cake isn't meant to look like a brick wall!"

Clearly seeing the red heat that Flora could feel flushing her face and neck, Jean stepped in diplomatically, "Well Betty, Flora has already explained that the loaves will still be stacked in tiers.

Besides, things have to change and move forwards. That's the way of life, even with weddings."

"Well, not in Baker's Rise, it isn't!" Betty harumphed and rearranged little Tina on her lap, her displeasure deliberately obvious.

"Didn't you yourself have that lovely, intimate service in the hospital chapel?" Sally asked pointedly, aware that she may be about to suffer Betty's wrath.

"Aye well…" Betty clucked her tongue against her teeth in displeasure but said nothing more on the subject, as an awkward silence descended – punctuated only by Reggie squawking, "Shut yer face!" in response to the tension in the room.

Flora stood abruptly and took the teapot downstairs to refill for the third time, wondering when the evening would ever end. She had already had to hide her phone in her handbag so that she wouldn't be checking it every five minutes to see if a message from Adam had come through, and even that had not helped her patience – or rather, the lack of it.

"Let me help you with that," Lizzie jumped up and held the door open. They were all gathered in the largest of the upstairs bedrooms, where everyone had been looking at the clothes, slipping to the room next door if they wanted to try any on. Lizzie was currently sporting a long tunic in a psychedelic lime and yellow swirling print, over her own black leggings.

"There's a large bangle that will match that dress perfectly," Flora said.

"Oh, I didn't realise there was jewellery?"

"Yes, two boxes of it, just metal and paste, nothing of any real value, I'll get it for you when we go back up," Flora offered, trying to stifle a yawn.

"That's great, thank you. So, how are you getting on with the Crawfords?"

"Well, they can certainly be… a handful," Flora admitted.

"Yes, I hoped they would be more professional for you," Lizzie's tone was apologetic.

"It's not your fault, Lizzie. To be honest, any mention of the wedding seems to be rubbing me up the wrong way at the moment."

They arrived in the kitchen, and Lizzie clearly decided to take the safer route and changed the subject, "So, I'll have the illustrations for book three finished by the end of the month. Have you found an agent yet?"

"No, I haven't had much time to enquire to be honest. It's looking more and more like I'll self-publish and I'm happy with that decision. I'll be able to sell the Reggie stories in the bookshop, and that was always my main intention."

"Sounds perfect then, you can go over the final proofs of the pictures after your honeymoon. Are you planning on going anywhere nice?" Lizzie added more milk to the vintage china jug and topped up the biscuit platter.

"Well, neither of us had any desire to go abroad, to be honest, and then of course there's Reggie to think about and the tearoom and bookshop, so we won't be able to go for longer than a week at most. Anyway, we've opted for a coastal town in Yorkshire – Lillymouth, it's called – as we cancelled our spring weekend away to that area when I hurt my ankle and then there was too much going on. Sally recommended the specific location as her friend has just moved in there as the parish vicar."

"Sounds lovely, it'll be just you and Adam and that's the main thing."

"Definitely, and after the wedding of the century I think we'll be glad of the peace and quiet," Flora placed the refilled teapot onto the tray with a rueful half-smile.

Back upstairs, Tanya had just tried on her fourth outfit of the evening, and was now wearing a figure-hugging vintage velvet ballgown in deep sea green. If she was using the opportunity to disappear into another room as a way to avoid chatting, none of the women seemed to notice.

"Oh, that necklace matches perfectly," Lizzie exclaimed as they reached the landing just as Tanya was emerging from the bedroom next door, "it looks just like... in fact I think it might actually be... Flora! Look! I'm pretty sure this is a real emerald!"

Flora deposited the tray back in the master bedroom and all the ladies gathered around Tanya, with Reggie flying over to take up sentinel duty on her shoulder. They peered at the square, green pendant, which was surrounded by no less than fourteen small, clear crystals, all of which reflected the light beautifully.

"It certainly catches the light," Amy peered at the necklace, rubbing her baby bump absentmindedly.

"Aye, and those little ones could be diamonds! Just look at them sparkle!" Betty said excitedly.

"Well, we probably shouldn't get our hopes up," Flora

found herself putting a damper on proceedings again, though she herself couldn't help but take a closer look.

"Well, that's as maybe, but imagine if they were real, you could afford to move into the big house here...."

"It's not just money that's holding me back, Betty, I simply haven't made a decision yet..." It was pointless continuing as the older woman's attention was already diverted back to the newly discovered treasure. Flora bit back a sigh.

Tanya smiled gracefully under all the attention, although the expression fell short of reaching her eyes, whilst Reggie seemed to think all the fuss was for him, and so puffed up his chest feathers, chirping "You sexy beast!" He leant down twice, trying to catch the gold chain in his mouth, only to be shooed back.

"We should go through the jewellery boxes!" Lizzie said excitedly, and all the women voiced their agreement.

"Okay then," Flora agreed, somewhat reluctantly, knowing this would extend the evening by at least another half an hour.

As Flora had thought, the top three quarters of each wooden box contained nothing but dress pieces, that were worth very little and had obviously been bought to complement particular outfits. Lizzie found the bangle to match her tunic and Shona found a string of painted bamboo beads to match the fuchsia pink jumpsuit she had chosen. Admittedly, Flora hadn't dug down to the bottom of the boxes before, and sure enough there was a removable shelf in each one, under which Tanya said she had found the necklace she was still modelling. Here they found dangly green earrings in the same square cut as the emerald pendant, again encased in what could potentially be diamonds, as well as a ring to match. Encouraged by the others, Tanya tried these on too. Still perched on her shoulder, Reggie seemed particularly enchanted by the hanging gem closest to him, batting it with his beak repeatedly until Flora removed him.

"It's not a toy, Reggie," she whispered, trying to avoid looking at the side-eye that the little bird was giving her in his displeasure.

"Flora stinks!" he exclaimed vehemently, flying up to perch on the doorframe.

On further investigation of the contents of the first box, there was, amongst others, an art deco style bracelet which looked to be decorated with deep blue sapphires, and a beautiful golden choker adorned with what could be rubies. All in all, as the women laid the antique pieces out onto the lid, there were a total of fifteen lustrous, heirloom-quality items found between the two boxes. Flora heard her own sharp intake of breath when she saw them set out in a row next to one another, their classic beauty and the quality of the gems quite evident now that she looked closely. Even the sulking Reggie had come down from his high perch for a closer look, trying to balance himself on the lip of the box lid and being shooed away by Hilda May.

"Aw, he's like a little magpie," Rosa joked, "he's clearly got an eye for quality!"

Hoping he wouldn't be noticed, Reggie flew immediately back to perch on Tanya's shoulder, slowly edging closer to the earring that was dangling irresistibly close to his beak.

"Desist! Silly bird!" Tanya whispered, moving him gently onto the bed cover and away from temptation.

"Bad bird!" Reggie shrieked at her unhappily, and Flora stroked his head to calm her little friend down, her mind whirring with possibilities. *Wasn't she the one to tell Betty not to get her hopes up? And now here she was…*

Lizzie offered to ask a friend in the antiques trade to come across from Alnwick and attest to whether the pieces of jewellery were, in fact, genuine, and if so then to value them. Flora agreed, figuring she might as well know one way or the other. When everyone had finally finished oohing and aahing, and all the scones and biscuits had been demolished, Flora asked for a small donation for charity for each outfit that was going home with a new owner, and was happy to close the door behind the last of her friends. Several had offered to help her clear up and then walk with her back to the coach house, but Flora was glad of the quiet distraction to calm her mind before heading home for the night.

What a long, unsettling day it had been and, checking her phone to see that there was still no word from her fiancé, Flora was glad to see the back of it.

SIX

"So you think I need a rhyming name for the shop?"
Rosa asked, as she sipped on her elderflower cordial.

She had only popped in with Matias to sign up for the
new weekly Baker's Rise Books and Butterflies toddler
sessions – a combination of story time and adventuring
in the estate grounds for pre-schoolers – and to thank
Flora for the enjoyable evening trying on clothes the
night before, but had been quickly invited by the
tearoom owner to join her and Betty for a quick cuppa.
Of course, Flora had no ulterior motives such as taking
Betty's attention off herself and redirecting it towards
the newcomer…

"Aye lass," Betty said decisively, whilst eying Rosa's
cold drink distastefully. When the new family had first
come to the village, the older woman had told Flora
repeatedly – and no doubt all of her friends in the W.I.

too – that she couldn't understand anyone not liking a good cup of hot tea. After all, she had said, there were plenty to choose from!

Sensing that Betty was going to begin these lamentations once again, and to Rosa's face this time, Flora jumped in, "When the Knit and Natter group first moved to the bookshop here, I suggested to Sally that it could be called Baker's Rise Hooks and Eyes – how about that name for the shop?"

"Oh, I like that," Rosa smiled widely and placed another piece of her banana bread onto the table in front of Matias, who was squirming on his big boy seat. They all watched as the chubby three year old gobbled it up in one mouthful, before even Reggie's keen eyes could spot the delicious morsel and swoop down from his perch. Like his mother, Matias had olive skin and dark curls, and he had his father's infectiously amenable temperament. The little boy was already a favourite with the Marshall girls and young Lewis, and with the adults alike.

"Such a canny bairn," Betty ruffled his hair fondly, "reminds me of when my Toby was a young'un."

"I haven't heard you mention him before, Betty. Is he your son?" Rosa asked.

"Aye lass, but this village was far too small for him. He upped and left as soon as he was out of high school. New Zealand the last I heard. He'll be in his late forties now though. I do get a Christmas card, mind you…"

"I'm so sorry," Rosa looked genuinely horrified that the memory might have caused Betty distress.

"Nay lass, I was always content to stay here, and so was my first husband. When I was widowed, it was even more reason to stick to the familiar, if you know what I mean."

"My grandmother is the same. I don't think she's ever travelled outside of the Andalucía region."

"Ah well, I did go on a grand adventure with my Harry last year. On a cruise ship of all things…" and Betty was off, regaling Rosa with her travels, and Flora let out a long, silent sigh of relief.

Distracted with saying goodbye to Betty, and to helping Rosa pry two books from Matias' sticky hands so they too could get on their way, Flora didn't notice the man who had entered the tearoom until she returned from the bookshop. She had heard the bell above the door, of course, but had expected it to be

Tanya arriving for her shift. Her friend was already half an hour late, which was completely out of character, and Flora had texted her once in that time to check that everything was okay. There had been no reply from Tanya, but instead Flora had received a rather worrisome message from Adam saying that he needed to speak with her urgently, not over the phone, and that he would come to the tearoom in an hour or so. Of course, this being the first communication since he had left abruptly the day before, Flora's mind started working overtime wondering what her fiancé could want to speak to her about that was so pressing. She hoped with all her heart that he didn't want to call off the engagement – but then, why else would the conversation have to take place face to face?

So Flora was especially distracted when she finally brought her attention to the man sitting waiting patiently at the table nearest the door. Reggie, she noticed, was eying him from a wary distance and the safety of his perch, his silence up to this point quite ominous, so Flora felt that she, too, should tread carefully.

The first thing that struck her were the tattoos. Never one to judge a book by its cover – or so Flora liked to think, anyway – she couldn't help but stare at the ink which adorned at least three quarters of the man's shaved scalp, winding its way down his face and neck to disappear beneath his shirt collar.

Flora gulped loudly, "Welcome to the tearoom!" She plastered what she hoped was a hospitable enough smile on her face and quickly pointed to the small, laminated menu.

"Just a coffee, please. Black," he had been polite enough, but something in those few words caused Flora to pause as she scribbled in her notebook. His accent? She wasn't sure, but something seemed familiar and Flora tried not to stare at the man again as her mind whirred trying to work out what it was.

"Is everything okay?"

"Sorry, yes, just a busy morning!" Flora felt her face flush as she scuttled back behind the counter like a mouse escaping a greedy cat. At least, that's how he made her feel.

Flora wondered if she should text Adam and ask him to come sooner, before mentally talking herself out of it. *She owned a café for goodness sakes*, she berated herself internally, *she needed to expect all manner of customers and not be a ridiculous schoolgirl about it!*

Perhaps her silent plea was heard after all, though, as

just as Flora was delivering the mug of strong black coffee – she felt that given the size of the man's hands, a mug would be preferable to one of her delicate, vintage china cups – Pat Hughes arrived with his police dog, Frank, in tow.

There was the usual kerfuffle as Reggie screeched in recognition and Frank bared his teeth briefly, though the regular, well-practised altercation between the two animals was brought to an abrupt halt by the newcomer scraping his chair back and standing up quickly as if in shock.

"Apologies," he muttered, "the animals..." he trailed off and sat back down, cradling the steaming mug of coffee with both hands, but Flora noticed that he didn't make eye contact with either Pat or Frank.

Pat himself seemed distracted, and Flora offered him a seat at the table closest to the counter, "What can I do for you, Pat?" Flora asked gently, as the man peered around behind her expectantly.

"I'm just here to have a quick word with my Tanya actually," Pat raised his eyebrows hopefully, "is she in the bookshop?"

"No, sorry Pat, she hasn't arrived yet. I tried to contact her, thinking maybe she was ill?"

"Ill? Nay lass, she left at the normal time. Wherever could she be? She's been acting awful off lately. Have you noticed? Quiet and subdued like?"

"I'm sorry, Pat, I've been... ah, too caught up in my own affairs if I'm honest," it sounded awful to Flora when she said it out loud, callous and uncaring. Tanya was one of her best friends, surely she should have noticed such a drastic change in temperament.

The local policeman ran his fingers through his hair absentmindedly and made a low whistling sound through his teeth, "I'll have to search for her then. Get Frank here on the case, I..."

Flora felt the eyes of the strange man behind her boring into the back of her head, and turned swiftly to see if he was indeed staring at her, just as the bell tinkled and Tanya walked in. She was without her usual dramatic flourish, to be sure, and ignored Reggie's greeting of "She's a corker!" Her signature red lipstick seemed to have been applied in haste, and Flora suddenly noticed the sunken, grey bags under her friend's eyes.

"Tanya, thank God," Pat rose quickly, his ample midriff catching on the table and almost sending it toppling as he rushed to hug his wife, "where have you been? Was it the doctor's? Are you poorly lass?"

"Ah yes, that was it, just some tablets for the… the migraine," Tanya managed a half smile and Flora didn't believe her for a minute. She couldn't imagine that Pat would be so easily fobbed off either, him being in the police force and all.

Whether he was truly convinced, or just didn't want to have the conversation in public, Pat simply brushed Tanya's bleached blonde hair back from her face gently and said, "Come back home, love, and sleep the headache off."

"Would that be okay, Flora?" Tanya's eyes were filled with tears.

"Of course, you go on – Pat, you make sure she gets there safely," Flora rubbed her friend's back, knowing that the 'normal' Tanya would never miss a day at work so easily. She had repeatedly told Flora how much she loved her job and their customers.

Nevertheless, now wasn't the time for that conversation, and Flora walked them to the door, realising only then that her strange visitor from earlier had left, a crumpled five pound note on the tablecloth all that remained to indicate he had ever been there.

SEVEN

Flora had no time to contemplate either what was bothering Tanya, or the unsettling customer, for just as she was closing the door behind them the sound of squealing tyres indicated that someone was coming up her gravel drive far too fast. Somewhat aghast to see Adam's familiar car screeching to a halt, Flora ran down the couple of steps to greet him as he got out of the vehicle.

"Adam? Is everything alright?" Though clearly, by the state of his driving, Flora could tell that was not the case. Nor did her fiancé look like he'd changed his clothes since the day before.

"Inside, love, is anyone else here?"

"No, why? I…"

"Let's lock the door and turn the sign to closed for a

few minutes, eh?" Adam guided Flora back into the
tearoom with his hand on her lower back, then turned
to check they weren't being followed and locked the
door, pulling the lace blind down over the little
window.

"Missed you!" Reggie squawked, though even he shut
up quickly when he sensed the mood.

"What's this all about, Adam?" Flora asked as soon as
they were sitting down, in the bookshop per Adam's
request so that no one could see them through the
windows, "Why so cloak and dagger? Is it to do with
what Blackett came to talk to you about yesterday?
You disappeared so suddenly, I..."

"Flora, love, could you take a breath?" Adam snapped,
and Flora immediately clamped her mouth shut,
feeling like a chastised child. "I'm sorry love, I'm..."
Adam reached out to take her hand, and Flora let him.
She wanted to withhold even that small touch, but
knew it would be churlish to do so.

She had missed something big happening in Tanya's
life, perhaps she had been blind to something
happening with Adam too? Flora decided to sit quietly
and let her fiancé speak. She ran her thumb in circles
over his palm and studied the man she loved carefully.

Adam was obviously trying to collect his thoughts, running his hands through his hair, which was longer than he usually kept it. Flora wondered randomly if he was waiting to visit the barber before the wedding. Their wedding. *Would there even be a wedding? Did she even want there to be one? What kind of bride put off buying her dress until the month of the event?*

"So, ah, yes," Adam eventually spoke, and when he did it was in a whisper which belied the fact they were the only ones in the building, "I've never told you about my family."

Though she was decidedly surprised by the abrupt mention of a topic that had seemed taboo whenever Flora tried to mention it before, she managed to nod and make a small noise of encouragement without actually saying anything.

"I grew up on the coast in North Yorkshire – Scarborough to be exact. My father was no father at all, an alcoholic who beat my mother into an early grave and almost killed my brother and I."

"Oh Adam, I'm so so…"

"Let me finish… let me finish," he whispered the repeat softly, "Carl is three years younger than me and I always tried to protect him. He was… headstrong. I'd hoped the old man's death in a drunken brawl would make him see sense, but no. Even when he got in with the gangs, with the drugs and then worse, I tried to get him to go clean. But I'd taken the opposite road. To protect and serve, to uphold the law. Inevitably, in the end, our paths collided. He was arrested for murder and sent down."

"My goodness. It wasn't you who arrested him?"

"No, it was Blackett, but we worked on some of the case together, and I'd already had enough dealings with the gang my brother was in to be a bit of a thorn in their side – shutting down their deals and suchlike, always trying to get Carl to see sense. Blackett's the only one who knows the story, and he came yesterday to tell me that Carl's been released from prison. He served fifteen years and now he's free, and, from what our informants on the street say, out for vengeance and already back with his old crew."

"He's coming after Blackett? Or you?" Flora couldn't help the quiver in her voice.

"Both probably," Adam looked utterly regretful, as if he wished he hadn't let that slip, "look love, it's a bit more complicated, because Blackett's been working on a big murder investigation that has ties to Northumberland, Tyne and Wear and Yorkshire, and

it's linked to the same gang – the Plamya cartel. It's a
Russian word which in English means The Flames.
They all have a single flame tattooed on the back of
their left shoulder. Sorry, you don't really need to
know that... Ah what I'm trying to say is that things
have become very messy, very quickly and I need you
to be aware, to be very aware so that you can keep an
eye out, and because I need to..."

"Yes?" Flora's stomach had that awful sinking feeling.
Was he about to call off the wedding? Even though she
knew that was such a selfish thought.

"Well, I'm not going to be around the village much
before our big day. You'll have to sort the rest of the
arrangements out yourself."

"Oh, oh okay," Flora felt the flush of relief, "okay.
Goodness me, I doubt he'd come to our small village
though, would he? How would he even know about
Baker's Rise? You live in Morpeth and I haven't visited
you there since we started wedding planning over
here."

"The group has their methods. Ones I'd rather not
share, love. Well, at least you'd know if he did show
up anyway – Big bloke, eyes same colour as mine, tats
all over his scalp..." Adam stopped abruptly when he
heard Flora's sharp intake of breath, "No, no, no,

you've seen him haven't you?"

"Just this morning, he was here, in the tearoom, I..."

"What did he say? Did he threaten you? Did you give him any information?" Adam stood abruptly.

"No! No, he barely spoke, I was with Pat Hughes at the time... and then he just left I think."

"You're not sure?" Adam dashed to the small bathroom and pulled open the door. Flora peered from behind him into the, thankfully empty, room. After another sweep of both shops, behind the counters and even in the deep space underneath the big coffee machine, where Flora stored her baking equipment and supplies, Adam returned to Flora, "I've got to speak to Blackett, don't open back up yet," and with that her fiancé rushed out to his car, making sure Flora locked the door behind him.

Flora didn't know quite what to do with herself. She typed a text message to Tanya and then deleted it without sending, deciding it would be better to speak to her friend in person. She listened to a voicemail from Lizzie, saying she had the number for the antiques dealer who specialised in jewellery and that they were free to come later that week if convenient. Flora made a mental note to reply later. Then there was another message, from Tammy Crawford this time, asking if she could call round to speak to her. Again, Flora put off replying. Her mind was whirring and she felt sick to her stomach. Even the little bird who had come to nuzzle in the crook of her shoulder and was chirping, "My Flora!" was doing little to calm her nerves.

Out of habit, Flora found herself behind the counter in the tearoom and putting the kettle on to boil. She prepared a mug with instant coffee granules for Adam, and put a chamomile teabag into a china cup for herself, then began wiping down the already sparkling countertops. The minutes ticked by.

Flora added the water to the cups and then carried them to the table by the door so that she'd be ready to unlock…

"Flora! Flora! Open up!" The hammering and shouting caught Flora off guard and she jumped, slopping her hot tea over the tablecloth.

"What is it?" she asked, as Adam pushed inside the moment the lock was undone, "What's happened?"

Adam took a deep breath, as if trying to calm himself

enough to speak, his trembling hands resting on Flora's shoulders as he leant forwards into her.

"It's Blackett. He's dead."

EIGHT

Flora could feel the fight leaving Adam's body as he sank into her, no doubt in shock, and she struggled to angle him onto the chair closest to them.

"Dead?" she heard herself squeak, her heart beating wildly in her chest, so clearly that she could hear it in her own ears. Surely she must've misheard… or misunderstood even.

Adam was sitting with his head in his hands, Flora's arms around his shoulders and her cheek resting against his as she bent down. He said nothing, only his muffled breathing could be heard and Flora wondered whether he was crying. She had never seen her fiancé so visibly upset, though he had come close when she herself had been hurt or threatened, and to see him like this increased her own panic tenfold. Rubbing his back gently, Flora forced herself to keep her mouth firmly shut and tried to infuse as much love and care as she could into her simple actions. Her unspoken questions raged inside and behind her Reggie fussed on his perch, waddling back and forth and clicking his tongue loudly in nervous agitation.

At length, Adam raised his face slightly, scrubbing at his eyes with balled fists, "Aye," he tried to say, but all that came out was a hoarse croak.

"Aye," he managed to speak on his second attempt, "shot in the head as he was leaving the station and walking to his car. Marksman, McArthur said, though I could barely hear her. I think she said she was only a few steps behind him."

"Adam, I'm so, so sorry," Flora whispered, sinking onto the chair beside him and wondering if she was actually going to be sick this time. She needed to be strong for him, so Flora swallowed twice and tried to think clearly.

"Well, obviously they'll need to keep you somewhere safe until they find the killer," Flora said, her mind working overtime and her main consideration being to keep Adam well away from harm. If she could, she knew she wouldn't let him out of her sight ever again. As it was, she knew his employers were best placed to protect him.

"What? No, love, it's my duty, mine, to find whoever did this to… my friend. And if it was my own brother… ye gods, Flora, I…" Adam's head sank into his hands once again and Flora tried unsuccessfully to hold back her own tears.

"No!" she whispered, though it came out more forcefully than she'd intended, "No, no, no, I need you. I need you safe. I love you, you can't…"

Adam stood abruptly, his chair scraping on the wooden floor, "Need to get out there, strike while the iron's hot, need to meet McArthur…" he was obviously talking to himself now, and shrugged off Flora's hand where she clung to his sleeve. As if suddenly remembering his fiancée was still there, Adam looked at Flora directly, through haunted, red-rimmed eyes, and said simply, "I'm so sorry, love," before unlocking the door swiftly.

He turned just before stepping outside and said, "I'll have Pat put on alert, tell him to keep an eye on you, and some uniformed officers sent up here too. Can you close up and hunker down at the coach house?"

"For how long? I mean, I..."

"Please, Flora," the stern tone was softened only by the edge of pleading and the look of love and desperation in Adam's eyes.

"Until we have more information, yes," Flora conceded, wanting nothing more than to reach out and pull him to her, to hold him to her chest and never let go.

But Adam had already left, the distance between them farther than the walk to his car. Much farther.

Flora locked the door and left the blind closed, turning to her feathered companion, her movements as if on autopilot.

"Reggie, Reggie, Reggie," she whispered, stroking his feathers and taking comfort in their silky softness.

"My Flora," he squawked in reply, tilting his head sideways and contemplating her studiously as if his small brain was trying to unravel a huge problem.

"Let's get cleared up and go home," Flora said, trying to keep her mind busy and off the mental picture of Blackett that was determined to stay front and centre.

"So cosy," Reggie chirped, accepting Flora's lift onto

her waiting shoulder and nuzzling in close.

Flora almost jumped out of her skin when there was a knock on the tearoom door just as she was putting on her cardigan to leave for home. Her first instinct was to ignore it and pretend there was no-one in the place, though this plan was soon scuppered by the little bird beside her who screeched, "Visitors! Visitors with money!" at the top of his lungs.

"Hush!" Flora scolded in a loud whisper, just as she heard a man's voice from outside.

"Flora? Flora, are you there? It's Gareth and Lewis!"

The air whooshed out of Flora on a huge sigh of relief and she stumbled forwards to unlock the door, being careful to raise the blind first to confirm that the welcome visitors were not accompanied by anyone rather more unwelcome.

"Gareth, I'm so sorry, I'm having to close early today… ah, family emergency."

"Nothing too serious I hope? Though we weren't actually after anything from the coffee shop…" Gareth began, as Lewis pulled on his arm to get him into the bookshop.

"I'm sorry, Lewis, the books are closed for today,"

Flora knelt down so that she was eye-to-eye with the boy. The tremble in his little lip caught her off guard and, feeling as emotionally fragile as she was, Flora almost burst into tears herself. "Oh!" she whispered, taking hold of his little hand, "Why don't we find something quick from the library shelf for you to borrow. There's a Thomas the Tank Engine book, I think."

"Thank you so much, Flora," Gareth was just about to follow them through, when Flora turned and indicated that he should lock the door behind him. If the man was surprised, he didn't say anything and just silently did as instructed.

Flora left Lewis to look at the books, and stood to face Gareth, Reggie on her shoulder squawking, "Secrets and Lies!" in her ear and causing her to feel even more flustered.

"So, Gareth, what can I do for you?" Flora caught herself wringing her hands and made a conscious effort to let them hang by her sides, only then noticing that Gareth himself looked decidedly uncomfortable. *I'm not surprised*, Flora thought to herself, *the way I've been acting all cloak and dagger since he arrived.*

"Well, I was wondering if, ah, if Lewis and I can borrow your rose garden later this week? I would need a little time one afternoon when the weather forecast is good, just to get everything set up, and then some time there in the early evening…" he trailed off, looking at Flora expectantly, and then down at Lewis, as if the moment had become too intense.

"Oh," Flora was surprised that the request was such a simple one. Nothing to be embarrassed about at all, "yes of course, little Matias loves playing hide and seek there when he and Rosa visit Laurie at lunchtime, I'm sure Lewis will love it!"

"Ah, well, that's not quite what I meant…" Gareth began, but Flora had already strode off to get her handbag from behind the counter in the tearoom. He led his son to the door with a rather perplexed look on his face, the little boy clutching a book to his chest as if he'd just found great treasure.

"Yes, any day he wants to play is fine by me, as long as it doesn't interfere with Laurie's pruning and whatnot," Flora spoke quickly as she and Reggie followed the two outside.

"Well, yes, ah thank you, Flora," Gareth scrubbed his hand over his face as Flora looked quickly up and down, scanning the driveway before checking the door was locked behind them and scurrying off in the direction of the coach house, totally oblivious that she'd completely missed the whole crux of the man's request.

NINE

Despite it being the summer, Flora couldn't help shivering as she let herself into her little coach house and bolted the door firmly behind her.

"We'll put the fire on, I think," she said to Reggie, though the bird was much more interested in the grapes she was getting from the fridge for him, her actions slow and sluggish.

"My Flora," he chirped contentedly, waddling up and down the counter and totally oblivious to the sobs which had begun to wrack Flora's whole frame.

"There, there, good bird," Flora whispered on a hiccough, more to herself than to her feathered companion.

As always, she was thankful for the comforting familiarity of her home, for the cosy sitting room with her favourite armchair always waiting, Reggie's large perch in the corner and the afternoon light streaming through the window. Flora's mind wandered to happy memories, to afternoons and evenings spent with Adam in this very room, and her tears redoubled their flow. Flora let them come, hoping that after she had got it all out of her system, and maybe found the energy to make herself a pot of chamomile tea, she would be able to think clearly and rationally again. Unfortunately, after twenty minutes of giving in to the emotion, all her crying gave her was a raging headache and a tight, uncomfortable feel to the skin on her face. The unsettled feeling, of anxiety and desperation, stubbornly remained.

When her phone began ringing from the kitchen, Flora nearly put her back out jumping up to race out and answer it, scrubbing at her face as she went and hoping with all her heart that it was Adam calling. Snatching up the source of the noise from where she had left it on the kitchen table, Flora felt a deep swell of disappointment to see Lizzie's name flashing on the small screen. Almost enough to tip her over the edge into weeping again, as her fingers fumbled with the buttons.

"Hello," it was all Flora could manage, and she knew she sounded as shaken as she was.

"Flora?"

"Yes, hi Lizzie, it's me."

"Are you okay? Maybe it's a bad line, you sound very quiet?"

"Just, ah, had a difficult day that's all. Received some bad news earlier so I've shut up shop and come home," Flora had no desire to expand further.

Luckily, Lizzie was sensitive and tactful enough not to press, "I can call back another time, Flora, it was nothing urgent, just the details for Marcus Fothergill, the antique gems dealer."

"No, go on, I need a distraction," Flora grabbed the notebook that was attached by a magnet to her fridge, and shooed away the little bird who hopped on her shoulder, hopeful that she might be of the mind to produce more fruit from the big metal box his grapes lived in.

"Okay, well I'll give you his mobile number. He says he's free tomorrow morning, but I'm not sure if that'll work for you…" The concern in the artist's voice was evident and Flora felt guilty for worrying her.

"Yes, I'll call him and say that's fine. I need all the distractions I can get at the moment. Hopefully Tanya will be feeling well enough to come back to the shop…" Flora trailed off, talking to herself as she tried to get her mind into gear.

"Would you like me to come round, give you some company?" Lizzie asked the question tentatively. It was a kind offer, especially as they were not really close friends.

"Ah, I appreciate it, but I think I'm best left with my thoughts today," it suddenly dawned on Flora that she was keeping the line busy when Adam might be trying to call her and so she rushed to finish the call, aware that she was being rather abrupt, "anyway, best fly."

"Oh okay, well you take care…" Flora hung up before she could hear the full sentence, scanning her phone to see if there had been any voicemail messages left while she was talking. Seeing none, the ball of worry in her stomach seemed to flutter and flail, making Flora feel extremely nauseous.

Holding the phone in a trembling hand, Flora brought up Adam's number on speed dial and hit call. *I need to know when I can leave the house,* she told herself as the call continued to ring out on the other end, *I'm perfectly entitled to call him.* Even though she knew he would likely be angry for the distraction, Flora didn't care enough to end the phone call, she just desperately needed to hear her fiancé's voice. His very much alive and well voice.

When it clicked through to voicemail, Flora hung up abruptly. The last thing Adam needed was a distraught message, muffled by her sobs – despite how much she was tempted to leave one, declaring her love, asking him to stay safe and to call her as soon as possible. Flora was actually quite proud of herself that she refrained from doing so, despite the additional ache it caused in her chest.

"Pipe down!" Reggie squawked from the comfort of his perch as Flora re-entered the sitting room, once again crying loudly. The bird had seed stuck to his face feathers, as if he had just dipped his whole head into the food bowl that was always topped up for his umpteenth snack of the day. His words may have been harsh, but Flora couldn't help a watery smile at the sight of him.

As if sensing he was the source of the slight lightening in her mood, Reggie puffed out his feathers and muttered a half-embarrassed, "Get out of it!" though there was no force behind his words, as he strutted up and down, seeds flying from his face in every direction.

"I guess I'll be sweeping the floor again," Flora whispered as she rubbed her wet face into the top of his downy head.

"You're my honey," Reggie chirped happily, apparently confident in the knowledge that he knew exactly how to butter his owner up.

The momentary peace was shattered, however, by a heavy knock on the front door and Flora almost jumped out of her skin for the third time that day. Tears of fear streamed silently down her face as she held her breath and tapped Reggie gently on the beak to encourage the little bird to follow her example and also stay silent. She prayed that whoever it was would give up and go away, chiding herself that she'd once again left her phone in the kitchen and so couldn't call Pat Hughes or even Adam for backup.

The seconds ticked by as if in slow motion, and the hammering ceased briefly. Flora slowly let out the breath she had been holding and was about to tiptoe to her chair – ridiculous, she realised, since the walls of this old place were so thick that the visitor, whoever they were, could not possibly hear her – when Reggie let out a shrill shriek of "Hide it all! Now there's trouble!" just as the knocking started up again.

"Argh, silly bird!" Flora shouted over the cacophony of sounds, marching to the front door without further thought and squinting her eye to look through the peephole.

TEN

"Oh my word, Pat, thank goodness it's you," Flora said as she pulled the door open and sent a quick prayer of gratitude heavenward.

"Aye, Flora, I rushed straight over here when I got Bramble's message, I've done a quick sweep of the village on the way up and haven't seen hide nor hair of any big bloke covered in tattoos, so there's that," he followed Flora inside, his trusty sidekick hot on his heels, "I'm sorry I didn't pick up on him when I was in the café, but I was too distracted about my Tanya..."

"Of course," Flora reassured him.

"Stay, Frank," the policeman ordered the burly canine in the hallway, and the dog sank down onto the narrow rug, though not before shooting his handler a look of extreme displeasure.

Reggie, who had swooped into the cramped space at the sound of the front door opening, came to an abrupt stop on the top of the kitchen door and shrieked, "Not that jerk!" three times, as if by doing so he could register his displeasure at having his space invaded by such a large, furry interloper. Frank himself barely seemed to notice the parrot's outburst this time, simply resting his head on his front paws, his eyes alert and constantly scanning the space around them. Flora guessed the difference in the dog's reaction was down to the fact he was on duty now, whereas he hadn't been when they'd popped into the tearoom.

His indifference seemed to wind Reggie up to new heights, however, and the bird began shrieking "Get out of it!" on repeat.

"Reggie, perch now," Flora ordered, down to her last drop of patience for the day.

"Aye well," Pat said, as if those two words alone could encompass the whole situation between the two animals.

"Indeed," Flora agreed, as she led the way into the sitting room, "Can I get you a drink, Pat?"

"Nay, it's all business, just wanted to check you were okay. I'll keep doing the rounds and I'll mek sure the guys sent over from the main station do the same, but I won't knock again, we'll just fade into the background."

"Thank you, I'm sure you've got much better things to be doing than babysitting me. Hopefully it won't be for very long… though I haven't heard from Adam … Oh! How's Tanya?" The question sounded like the afterthought that it was, and Flora felt awful – how could she have forgotten to ask after her friend?

A look of concern clouded Pat's face and he shuffled his policeman's helmet from one hand to the other distractedly. His lengthy pause before answering ratcheted Flora's anxiety up another couple of notches until she felt it was almost unbearable to contain.

"You say you've noticed no change in her?" Pat asked, as if simply continuing their conversation from earlier.

"I'm so sorry, Pat, I've had a lot on my mind, what with the big house and the wedding…" Flora heard it for the pathetic excuse it was, though Pat didn't show any sign of annoyance.

"Understandable, lass, understandable, it's just she's… that lie this morning, I don't think it's the first, though I'm pretty sure she'd always given me the truth up to a couple of weeks ago."

"It's so unlike Tanya, Pat, I know how much she values the honesty and trust that's between the two of you. Which makes me imagine it must be something very serious," Flora wanted nothing more but to dissolve in tears again. Given the way the local policeman had eyed her blotchy, swollen face warily when he'd arrived, and then chosen not to pass either comment or question on it, she was pretty sure he wouldn't be very comfortable with her breaking down now. So, Flora simply bit her lip and tried to slow her breathing as she waited for him to respond.

"Aye, that she does, I'm sure of it. No point sitting wallowing in my worries, though, is there? I'm going to have to do some investigating of my own, I think, maybe follow her when she gets up. Not that I think she's actually got a migraine, mind you, though I suppose it could be a tension headache. She's gone to ground now, snuggled up in bed like she wants to forget there's a whole world outside the door. So unlike her…" his voice was rough with emotion.

"She normally grabs life with both hands," Flora agreed, conjuring a mental image of her larger than life friend in a gaudy floral velvet jumpsuit she had tried on at the weekend.

Pat grunted his agreement and stood abruptly, causing

Reggie to become agitated once again.

"There'll be hell to pay!" he shrieked, causing Frank to rush in from the hallway, ears pricked up and alert for danger.

"Enough!" Flora shouted, rather more loudly than the situation warranted, before clamping her mouth shut and shaking her head at Pat in an expression of utter defeat.

"I'll be off," the girthy policeman seemed to fill the whole width of the hallway as Flora followed him to the front door, Frank padding ahead quickly as if he couldn't wait to be free of the place, "call me if you need any help at all. Any time, Flora, I'm serious."

"Will do."

"Good riddance!" Reggie shrieked after them, and Flora was about to tell him to go to his cage there and then when she heard the familiar tone of her phone ringing from the kitchen.

"Adam!" Flora practically shrieked his name into the device, her heart thumping loudly in her chest.

"Aye love, I wanted to see if you're okay, I saw I'd

missed a call from you earlier."

"Yes, I just, I just… needed to hear your voice. Are you alright?"

"Aye, as well as can be expected. They've launched a big manhunt for Carl, though we have no evidence it was even him that kill… that got Blackett."

"Is McArthur okay? Pat's just been. I'm in the coach house…" Flora tried to get everything out in one breath before he went again.

"She's been sent home, you can imagine how distraught she was. We all are. I'm staying on duty till they find the killer… whoever or whenever that may be. I'm glad Pat has been round. You need to stay safe love. For me. For us."

"I know. I will. I love you," Flora tried to swallow down the huge lump in her throat.

"I love you too, I'll call round… maybe tomorrow if I can… we need to talk about… about upcoming events," Flora had no confusion as to what he was referring to, and the hesitancy in Adam's voice told her everything she needed to know about the direction their wedding plans were taking in light of the recent tragedy.

Surprising herself, she found she didn't even care. What she wanted was the man she loved, safe and well, and here beside her – she wasn't bothered about the big wedding any more. *Had she ever been?*

"Look love, don't even think about the wedding, consider it postponed," Flora's confidence in her decision grew the moment she voiced it.

"Aw love, we can talk about it, it's just..."

"Shhh, I know, and I understand completely. It was getting too big anyway. Turning into something neither of us wanted. Really, I'm fine with it."

"You're not just saying that?"

"No, I'm not actually, I feel... freer knowing we've made the decision."

Adam sighed, a shuddering sound that was a mixture of relief and affection, "I love you, Flora, I want you to be my wife."

"I will be, just not in three weeks' time."

"Look, I've got to go, but you stay safe, you hear me?"

"Yes, but can I go up to the big house? I'll need to cancel the arrangements, and there's an antique dealer and..."

"Straight from the coach house to the manor, and take Reggie with you. He'll let you know if there's anyone skulking around."

"Okay will do. Come and see me as soon as you can, I need to hold you," Flora's voice cracked and she knew it was time she stopped speaking. The poor man needed all his wits about him, and Flora knew she was a distraction he couldn't afford at the moment.

"Love you," he whispered and then he was gone, and so was Flora's resolve.

The tears cascaded down her cheeks like a waterfall and she was grateful for the feel of soft feathers against her neck.

ELEVEN

After scurrying up the path, her nerves on edge and feeling every bit as if she herself was the criminal, Flora had made it to the manor house early the next morning. Out of breath, her face red hot and sweating, she had been glad of the cool welcome the old house gave her. Locking the back door and opening the windows a crack to let more fresh air in, Flora had been glad to reach her destination without being accosted by either friend or foe. Now, as she sat with her cup of morning coffee at the kitchen table in one of the workmen's mugs, wishing she could go outside and enjoy it sitting on Billy's bench instead, Flora wondered why she had hurried up so early in the day.

Ah yes, she remembered then, as if her mind had deliberately blocked it out, *to cancel all the wedding suppliers*. Not that the thought of doing so upset her, it was more the uncomfortableness of the whole thing that Flora wished she could avoid. Realistically, the Crawfords would handle most of it, it was just the vicar and the wedding planners themselves that Flora would have to deal with directly. Reggie was already on his perch in the study, having his second breakfast of the day, when Flora heard voices approaching outside, the sound wafting through the open windows.

Her first instinct was to duck and hide, until common sense prevailed and she listened harder, recognising Laurie's cheerful voice and that of a woman, as they paused outside the back door.

"I shouldn't have come so early, but I've barely slept, and when she wasn't at the coach house, my feet just seemed to bring me up here," Flora craned her neck to hear, deducing that the voice certainly didn't sound like that of Laurie's wife, Rosa.

"I'm sure she won't mind, but did you check the tearoom? That's normally where she's to be found," Laurie replied kindly.

"I'm here," Flora opened the door suddenly, startling them both, "Oh! Hello Tammy! I was just thinking that I needed to call you."

"Really? Ah well, my visit isn't exactly about the wedding... it's a bit personal actually," Tammy fidgeted with the strap of her handbag as she shuffled her foot in the gravel, the dust rising around her sandaled toes in a small cloud.

"Well, ah, I'm off to trim the hedges in the ornamental gardens," Laurie tipped his cap and made a quick exit. *Sensible man*, Flora thought, not relishing the prospect of a heartfelt discussion herself at this time in the morning. She'd have to tell her gardener that the mad hurry to get everything ship shape in time for her nuptials was off, but for now Flora turned her concentration to the woman in front of her.

"So, what can I do for you?" Flora asked, rather hesitantly, when she and Tammy were seated in the cosy study room, with Reggie having been sent to his perch after a particularly ear-splitting rendition of "She's a corker!" followed quickly by "You sexy beast!"

Tammy had been so preoccupied that she had barely noticed the parrot's outburst, but it had grated on Flora's already-frayed nerves and she had snapped at her little feathered companion. Now she sat expectantly, feeling rather guilty and hoping the younger woman would start talking soon. Aware of the repeated flick of little seeds as they ricocheted off her back and neck, Flora pursed her lips and tried hard to ignore the physical reminders of her bad mood.

"Tammy, is everything okay?" Flora tried again, a kinder undertone to her voice this time.

"Sorry, Flora, I'm just thinking of the best way to say this. I was planning it in the car all the way here, and yet now the right words are escaping me."

Flora tried to be patient, she really did. She smoothed the skirt of her pretty sundress over her knees, glared at the little bird who was now looking like butter wouldn't melt, and turned back to her guest. Still nothing.

"Take all the time you need, I'll just go through and pop the kettle on," Flora rose, just as Tammy blurted out.

"It's Micah, I'm still in love with him! He's changed his number since we were together, but I wondered if you could get a message to him for me?"

"Micah?" Flora stalled for time, though she knew her guest was referring to Blackett. The two had certainly seemed to be caught up in an emotional reunion the other day – until Tammy's father had brought the moment to an abrupt end, that is. The bile rose in Flora's throat, knowing as she did that news of the detective's death had not been made public yet.

"Yes, Micah Blackett and I were engaged this time two years ago," there was an impatience in her visitor's voice now, as if she assumed Adam would have filled Flora in on the details. He hadn't, of course. He'd had much bigger things on his mind since the encounter at the weekend.

"I, ah, I didn't know that. I wasn't in the area at the time," Flora walked over to her desk and began rearranging the already tidy papers – anything to give her shaking hands a focus, "and it didn't end well?"

"No, and not by my choice. He ran a police search on my father, found out he'd been 'made redundant' due to allegations of fraud and then arson – none of which could be proved despite a police investigation – and then told me that although he still retained strong feelings for me, he couldn't be tied to someone with a criminal family," Tammy's voice rose in pitch and desperation, until Flora found herself sitting alongside her visitor on the couch, holding the woman's hand in an attempt to calm her.

"Well, I didn't know him well, but he did seem a stickler for conformity, with very high standards and as if once his mind was made up it couldn't be changed," Flora looked up to see Tammy staring at her with wide, questioning eyes.

"Why are you talking about him in the past tense?" Tammy whispered.

"I, ah..." Flora could have kicked herself, or quite happily pitched a tent in Baker's Bottom and lived there as a recluse, to avoid this and all other conversations. As it was, she had dug her own hole.

Telling Tammy was one thing, and the woman could surely be sworn to secrecy, but more importantly Flora had not intended to let the news of Blackett's death slip in such a heartless way. There was no choice now, however, but to let the poor woman know as gently as she could.

"Well, I'm so sorry to have to tell you this, but Micah Blackett was killed yesterday. Murdered outside the station."

"No! You must be wrong!" Tammy flew out of her seat, upsetting Reggie who had been keeping a quiet eye on proceedings. He flew from his perch, straight to Flora's shoulder, and sat there as if on guard duty. Their visitor began pacing the room, dragging at her hair until it slipped out of the band that was holding it up in a ponytail, "He couldn't have... he wouldn't have... what has my foolish father done now?" she muttered to herself like a woman possessed.

"Let me get us some tea, you can talk about... ah it all," Flora said, rising once again to go to the kitchen, hoping to distract the woman from her accusatory ravings. Flora certainly didn't want to get caught up in wondering if there was any other suspect for Blackett's death than the ones Adam was focusing on.

"No need," Tammy pushed past her, heading straight for the back door, "I'm going to the station in Morpeth to find out everything I can!"

"I'm not sure that's a good idea..." Flora began, but her guest had already unlocked the back door, tears streaming down her face, and her eyes wild with a mixture of grief and disbelief.

Woman and bird watched their guest fleeing back around the front of the house, on her way to where her car was presumably parked down near the tearoom, until Flora thought to hurry back into safety and lock the door firmly behind them. Her own tears had begun again in earnest, and she realised as she finally managed to fill the kettle that she hadn't even told Tammy that the wedding had been cancelled.

What a mess, Flora thought sadly, *what a tragically awful mess*.

TWELVE

Relieved to receive a text from Tanya saying that she had opened the tearoom – despite Flora having already messaged that she shouldn't rush back if she was feeling under the weather – Flora quickly replied giving a description of the man that she should keep an eye out for. The one everyone was looking for – Carl Bramble. It turned out that Pat had already filled his wife in, and was currently there with her, pretending to take an hour to drink one cup of tea and, according to Tanya, 'driving her mad with his suffocating care.' It made Flora happy to know that her friend was being well looked after and her chest felt a bit lighter for the first time in days.

Stalking up and down the large hallway, her legs

itching for a distraction and something to fill the time until Mr. Fothergill arrived for the meeting regarding the vintage jewellery, Flora typed in the number for the vicarage and waited impatiently for an answer. Her kitten heels clicked on the tiled floor as her pacing continued, and Flora was just about to give up and try later when a very breathless-sounding Sally answered.

"The Vicarage. Hello?"

"Hi Sally, it's Flora."

"Flora, thank goodness, I thought it might be the Bishop," the squealing shrieks of two young girls arguing in the background could clearly be heard, as Sally raised her voice to be heard over them, "the school summer holidays began this week, and we're all adjusting to being with each other every day."

Flora thought that was a rather diplomatic way of putting it, as was Sally's talent, since it wasn't yet ten in the morning and it sounded like all hell had broken loose down there, "I'm sorry, it's not a good time, I can call back later," Flora offered, "or better yet, perhaps you could come to the coach house for a cuppa? Give you a break when James is finished for the day."

"You know what, Flora, right now that sounds like heaven. Just an hour out of the house by myself."

"I'll see you later then, early evening?"

With plans in place, Flora hung up and was about to go outside for some fresh air, when she suddenly remembered her current predicament.

"Argh!" she groaned, to no-one in particular, going through to the large, front room just in time to see two uniformed officers walking back down the driveway. They must've been doing a sweep of the place, and Flora was glad a certain feathered friend hadn't spotted them.

As it was, her impromptu exhalation of displeasure had her little companion flying swiftly through from the study, his eyes on alert.

"My Flora!" he squawked, landing on her arm.

"It's fine Reggie, just sick of being stuck in already," Flora tried to sound reassuring, even though the dark cloud that surrounded her felt like it was choking the words from her throat. And there wasn't enough tea in the whole of China to soothe it at the moment.

At eleven o'clock on the dot the heavy lion's head knocker on the main door was rapped twice in quick succession, followed by silence. Flora inwardly thanked the man who stood on the doorstep for having the patience to not keep knocking, as her head was already beginning to throb with the tension and worry of the day.

To say the antiques dealer was not what she expected would be an understatement. Flora had presumed he would be an older gentleman, perhaps with mutton chop sideburns, a penchant for tweed waistcoats, an expensive, gold, antique pocket watch, and beady eyes that missed nothing under an overly jovial fake façade.

As it was, the man that stood in front of her now looked to be in his thirties, tall and broad, dressed in black jeans and a rock band logo'd tee-shirt that did little to hide his gym-built physique. To add to the effect, he was just shrugging his arms out of a leather biker's jacket. Given that he had arrived at the exact moment of their pre-arranged appointment, Flora realised that she had stupidly forgotten to look through the spy hole before swinging the door wide open.

Her legs shaking, her breath coming in short gasps, she was about to beat a hasty retreat, slamming the door in the stranger's face, when the man held out a tattooed arm and said, "Marcus Fothergill. Call me Marc."

"Oh, ah, Flora, Flora Miller, pleased to meet you,"

Flora didn't realise she was still staring at the man, frozen to the spot and clutching his hand in hers in an embarrassingly long handshake, until Reggie began to circle above them. He had obviously restrained himself up till now, but sensing Flora's hesitance he divebombed the stranger, shrieking, "Get out of it! Stupid git!"

His reaction brought Flora back to her senses. She felt ridiculously silly, her mind being so quick to judge the man based simply on his appearance. Though, to be fair, it was rather close to that of the man the police were hunting. Nevertheless, her body seemed to have been frozen in place with the shock of it and she blinked up into deep brown eyes that were filled with nothing but concern.

"Reggie! Perch or cage!" Flora spoke on autopilot, recovering her errant hand and placing it on her hip. Neither of them spoke again until the sulking parrot had shrieked "Bad bird!" three times, presumably at Flora but it could have equally been angled towards their guest, before leaving the porch and tearing down the hallway in a flurry of feathers.

"I'm so sorry," Flora spoke softly, "It's been ah... a difficult couple of days."

"I'm sorry to hear it. Is now still a convenient time to

look at the jewellery? I could come back…"

"No, no, now is as good a time as any. I'm on house arrest anyway."

To his credit, the man simply raised a surprised eyebrow at her admission, and followed Flora silently to the kitchen, where she had laid the pieces out on the kitchen table to catch the best of the morning light on that side of the house.

Marc accepted her offer of a cup of coffee and began sifting through the jewellery as Flora made them both drinks.

"So," he said as she joined him at the table, "tell me again how you found these."

Flora explained about the vintage clothes sale, and about Tanya finding what they believed was an emerald and diamond set, though when she scanned the table she couldn't find the pieces in question.

"Oh! Perhaps I've left them upstairs," Flora muttered, somewhat embarrassed, and sure in herself that everything had been stored back in the jewellery box after the event. She certainly hadn't taken them out since, what with everything that had been going on, but trudged upstairs to look anyway, leaving her visitor downstairs and praying that Reggie didn't choose that moment to come looking for them.

"Any luck?" Marc asked as she re-entered the kitchen, a magnifying glass in his hand as he held what looked like a sapphire brooch up to his eye.

"No, sorry, I've no idea, unless…" A sudden thought struck Flora and she raised her voice, "Reginald Parrot get in here!"

If Marc thought her outburst strange he said nothing, her increasingly exasperated breathing the only thing that could be heard until Flora repeated the phrase and at length the beating of wings could be heard approaching the room.

When the parrot appeared, having knowingly kept them waiting and clearly still sulking, he went straight to sit on the counter, making no eye contact with Flora.

"Reginald Parrot," she said sternly, picking up a gold and opal pendant and carrying it over to the bird, "do you have any of these pretties? Are you masquerading as a magpie now?" As if she needed one more thing to deal with.

Of course, Reggie probably had no idea what his companion was saying and instead seemed to interpret her actions as Flora offering him the jewellery as a peace offering. He lurched forward, trying to grasp the dainty item in his beak, and Flora only just pulled her hand back in time.

"Well, I think that is all the proof we need," Flora turned to Marc, feeling the heat of embarrassment on her face, though her stomach roiled at the thought of Reggie stealing things from under her nose. The notion simply didn't sit right.

"Not to worry, I can look those over when you, ah, recover them," Marc said, smiling kindly, "I can tell you just by looking at these other pieces that you've got quite the haul here. Really, it's spectacular. I've personally never seen so many antique finds together in one lot."

"Really?" Flora felt her legs shaking – for a completely different reason this time – and slid into the nearest chair, "I mean, are you saying they're worth something."

"Not just something, Mrs. Miller, a whole heck of a lot of something!"

THIRTEEN

Still reeling from Marc's appraisal at least half an hour after he left, Flora was startled from her musings by her phone.

"Flora lass, it's me, Betty…"

"Yes Betty, your name flashed up…" Flora gave up trying to explain to Betty how mobile phones worked, and instead stood silently as the older woman launched into the reason for her call.

"It's young Gareth, he's just walked past with little Lewis. Looks awful nervous. To be expected, I know. He came round here last evenin' and asked Harry for a bit o' advice like. Anyway, wanted to give you the heads up. Perhaps you can offer them some tea and cake when he's set it all up, put him at ease an' everything."

"At ease? For playing hide and seek?" Flora was perplexed.

"Eh?" Evidently, so was Betty.

A moment of uncomfortable silence dragged out, and Flora took the phone with her to find Reggie in the study. He was still sulking, although he did follow her back through to the kitchen – in the hope of a conciliatory grape or two no doubt!

"Anyway," Betty chose to plough on regardless, "don't let him change his mind!"

"Right then," Flora knew it was pointless to argue and decided to assume the confusion was all Betty's. Perhaps she had Gareth mixed up with someone else.

"All okay?" Betty asked, perhaps detecting the reticence in Flora's tone to commit fully to the conversation.

"Well, er…"

"I'll tek that as a no then, lass. Anything we can help with?"

Not wanting to tell Betty the true cause of her worries,

Flora filled her in on the visit from Marcus Fothergill and her suspicions about Reggie. She left out the eye-wateringly large sums he'd mentioned before he'd taken numerous photos of the whole box full of jewellery so as to make a proper evaluation from his office.

"No, not that little chap," Betty had a soft spot for Reggie, almost as much as Flora herself did, "I know he can be feisty and has a bit of a cheeky beak on him at times…"

"That's an understatement if ever I heard one!"

"Aye well, I know that, but taking things he shouldn't? When he could tell it would mek you mad with him? No, Flora lass, that doesn't sound right to me."

"I know, me neither," Flora sighed down the line, "I just don't want to think of the alternatives – that either I've lost some very valuable, precious items, or one of the ladies from the clothes sale has light fingers."

"What? No! We're all friends the lot of us!" Betty was aghast at the suggestion.

"Exactly, so it's either the parrot or my own error, but I'm sure I packed them all away Betty."

"Totally sure?"

"Well, I didn't watch them all going into the box the other night, but I haven't touched it since."

"Hmm," Betty's displeasure came through the phone, and although Flora knew it wasn't aimed at her, it still made her hackles rise.

"Anyway, busy day, so I'd better get going."

"Aye lass, only a few weeks till the big day. Harry and I couldn't be prouder, you know, and that silly man is already all emotional about walking you down the aisle."

Flora swallowed down the lump that Betty's kind words created and tried to talk through the stifling emotions that swelled up in her chest, "Thank you Betty, I ah, well, whatever happens know that I love you and Harry."

"Whatever happens? What do you mean, lass? What's going to happen..?" Flora had no choice but to hang up before her friend heard the sobs that she could no longer choke back. Loud and demanding attention, her emotion consumed her, so much so that Reggie flew to the back door, clearly trying to get out to alert someone to Flora's distress.

Lucky – or unlucky – for them, it was at that very moment that Gareth and little Lewis arrived at the back of the house. Flora heard their footsteps on the gravel and Lewis chattering away as she tried desperately to calm her breathing.

"My Flora! My Flora!" Reggie screeched from behind the closed door, as if trying to get their attention.

Flora sensed the moment Gareth heard the bird, as his footsteps faltered, and where she assumed he had planned to walk straight past the back door and on to the rose garden, he now stopped and knocked tentatively.

"Welcome to the tearoom!" Reggie shrieked, flying to Flora and back to the door again in sweeping circles.

"Yes, yes, silly bird," Flora muttered as she made her way to pull the bolt back and greet their visitors.

"Oh, hello Flora. Sorry to bother you, I wasn't going to knock, but er…" Gareth looked at her with a compassion-filled gaze, and Flora could only imagine what he saw. A middle aged woman with her eyes and nose still streaming, hardly lady of the manor material.

"Why crying?" Lewis looked at her with horror and worry written across his little face, "She crying, daddy!"

"I know son, perhaps we should leave Mrs. Miller in peace and come back another day."

"No daddy! It's big surprise for our Amy!" Lewis shook his father's hand which he was holding, yanking it up and down in frustration.

"Why don't you both come in for some tea and cake, and you can tell me about this surprise?" Flora pulled the door open wider.

"No, we wouldn't want to impose," Gareth shook his head to emphasise his refusal just as Lewis dragged him inside the doorway.

Flora gave a watery smile as Gareth let out an exasperated sigh, mouthed 'sorry' to her and let himself be pulled inside by the determined four year old.

"Reggie birdie!" Lewis shouted when he spied the parrot, running straight over to where the bird sat on the table top and holding out his arm.

"Really, Flora, we can come back," Gareth looked about as awkward as a man can get, and it was just then that Flora noticed his free hand had been holding a bunch of balloons and flowers. Finally, it began to dawn on her that the visit wasn't for a play date at all, and that Betty had been right all along.

"Are you planning to..?" Flora let the question hang in the air as she indicated Gareth should take a seat at the farmhouse style table.

"Propose. Yes," his face turned even redder at that, and Flora felt for the man.

"I'm so happy for you, Amy will be thrilled!"

"Do you think? I mean, the pregnancy is making her tired and I've been working to earn all the money I can before the baby comes, and I should've done this a lot sooner. She's due in a couple of months and I really wanted us to be married before that. Not that there's time enough now…" he trailed off, tapping his index finger on the table and watching as the balloons tried to struggle free where he had them pinned under the enormous bouquet in front of him.

Flora felt for the man, knowing his history of how he had lost his first wife and seeing how he was clearly struggling now, "I've got to know Amy quite well, what with her working a little in the bookshop, and I'm sure she just wants to be with you and Lewis. Yes, I'm pretty certain she would love a ring on her finger, but really she just wants you all to be happy together."

Flora felt the tears beginning again and turned abruptly to the counter, busying herself getting out cups and saucers, china plates and the remains of a Victoria sponge cake. Lewis and Reggie were charging up and down the hallway, and Flora heard Gareth clear his throat uncomfortably.

"Oh, I almost forgot," Gareth began, changing the subject completely, "I met your new handyman out front there."

"Laurie? Well he's really the gardener, expert with plants, I'm very lucky to have him."

"Huh? Well, I have to say he's not what I expected. Amy mentioned he and his wife have a little boy who could become a friend for Lewis, but having seen the man I'm not so sure."

Flora turned to face him then, her eyebrows raised and the turmoil in her stomach starting up again, like a washing machine that had simply been paused mid cycle, "Really? And why is that?"

"Well, ah, what with the shaved head and tattoos, and the way he barked at us to get out of his way…"

The crash of Flora dropping the cake plate reverberated through the room and she felt her legs give way beneath her. The scrape of Gareth's chair was like a distant rumbling and although she felt his arms holding her up, it was as if she was detached from the whole experience.

Clearly, it was one shock too many for her feeble brain to compute and her weary body had followed suit. Flora simply gave up trying to fight it.

FOURTEEN

"Flora! Flora!" Gareth's voice sounded as if he was at the other end of a very long tunnel and it was a struggle for Flora to search through the mental darkness to reach him.

In the end, it was the shrieking of "My Flora!" and the feel of soft feathers against her face that brought Flora round. Not that she really wanted to face the present, but she had little choice in the matter.

"Gareth? I'm so sorry, I…" Flora could feel his strong arm still around her waist.

"No, no need to apologise, let's get you sat down here," Gareth manoeuvred her to a chair at the table, not letting go till he was certain Flora wasn't going to pass out again.

"I'm fine, really, thank you," Flora could feel the embarrassment heating her face, though she was well aware that was the least of her worries in this moment.

"Can I get you a glass of water, or…"

"Can you phone Pat Hughes? Ask him to get up here as fast as he can… and to bring Frank."

"Of course," Gareth moved to make the call on his mobile, little Lewis clinging to his legs as if the boy could sense the sudden tension.

Flora sat with her elbows on the table, her head in her hands, trying to regulate her breathing. Her brave feathered friend had taken up guard duty in front of her, waddling up and down the table, his little eyes alert for danger.

"Good bird," Flora whispered. Her mind was whirring but at the front of it all she knew that she must call Adam and let him know that his brother had been at The Rise not half an hour ago. Not surprisingly, the call went to his voicemail, so Flora left a rather curt message, not trusting herself to speak for longer in case she spewed out everything that was on her heart.

"I'll wait in here until Pat arrives," Gareth said,

finishing his phone call with the local policeman and resuming his seat on the other side of the table, "I'm guessing the bloke I saw is not an employee?"

"Not at all, no, I'm sorry I can't say…"

"Of course, of course. I'm so grateful to you for letting me use the rose garden… and that new bath I plumbed in for you the other week looks a picture. Very fitting for the period of the property it being standalone with clawed feet…" and with that the kind man started speaking about anything and everything he could think of to take Flora's mind off her current predicament.

With a speed that Flora didn't know the man possessed, Pat Hughes arrived very shortly afterward, his face red and sweating and his breath laboured. That wasn't what shocked Flora though – no, what made her own breath catch in her throat was the man who was being shepherded through the back door in front of the pot-bellied policeman, a growling Frank bringing up the rear.

"Vic!" Flora exclaimed.

"I'm all shook up!" Reggie shrieked, the sight of the

floor fitter obviously triggering his memories of his
Elvis fascination, "Caught in a trap... can't walk out..."

"Reggie!" Flora scolded, her patience non existent
despite her gratitude for the little bird's care.

"I take it you know this man?" Pat asked, "I found him
skulking out front. Doesn't match the description...
apart from the tattoos up his arms, but still..."

"Yes, yes, he was on the team who fitted my floors up
here recently."

"I was just coming to return the book... the tearoom
and bookshop were all locked up..." Flora heard the
nervous stammer in Vic's voice and sympathised with
the man.

"Oh! I thought Tanya was in the shop?" she spoke
more to herself than any of the men, "Please let him go,
Pat, he was just in the wrong place at the wrong time, I
think,"

"I'm right sorry I am," Vic was wringing his hands
together, as Pat loosened his hold on the man's arms,
"I hovered out front cause I didn't know if I should
knock like, wasn't sure what to do since I'm not
working up here anymore... grand house like this..."

"It's fine, Vic, really. Once I've, ah, dealt with

everything I'll open the book shop and you can get a few new reads. It'll probably not be today though, sorry."

"Not at all, I'll come back another day," the man had turned and scarpered back out the door before he'd finished speaking, and Frank gave three loud barks to send him on his way.

This set Reggie off again, and the bird jumped straight back in with the song lyrics, "I love you too much... baby."

Talking over him, and giving her feathered friend the same look which every angry mother seems to perfect, Flora stood on shaky legs and then smiled at Gareth, "Thank you so much, I'm sorry I interrupted your special plans."

"Not at all, no problem, the main moment will be this evening anyway... all being well..." Gareth retrieved his flowers and balloons, and held his hand out for Lewis. The boy himself was reluctant to leave, seemingly in heaven having a real life policeman and police dog in the same room. He was currently lying across Frank's furry back, the dog doing nothing to shake him off, as if he hadn't just been the snarling professional canine who'd escorted poor Vic in from outside.

"So," Pat said when he and Flora were alone apart from the animals, "I'm not sure I want to leave you up here, Flora. Can I walk with you back down to the coach house? Then I'll do a detailed sweep of the estate and the village."

"Yes, thank you, Pat, I'm hoping Adam will meet me there when he gets my message," Flora chewed the inside of her cheek, trying desperately not to get upset again, "Oh! Do you know why Tanya would've locked up the shop?"

"No lass, I was just wondering that myself," a cloud of sadness had fallen over the man's features, and Flora wondered if perhaps he knew something that she didn't.

"Is she... okay?" Flora wasn't sure she could take any more bad news right now, though if her friend had received a worrying medical diagnosis or suchlike then Flora certainly wanted to know about it so that she could offer support – what little capacity she had left, anyway.

"Well, I ah..." Pat seemed to come to a decision as he patted Frank's head absentmindedly, "Has she mentioned anyone to you... any other man?"

"You think she's having an affair?" Flora realised her

111

voice had risen significantly in pitch and so took a deep breath in, disbelief no doubt written across her face.

"I'm not sure, truthfully, it's just she keeps disappearing off, and when she comes back she's so distant… She's aloof all the time if I'm honest, but especially after."

"I'll speak to her Pat, I promise, we need to get to the bottom of it. She obviously needs help… for something. But adultery? No, never! I've heard the way she talks of you with such affection."

"I know, I know, I trust her, I love her," the man's voice broke on the last gruff word and Flora reached out to squeeze his arm through his uniform jacket, "Anyway, let's get you home."

"Thank you, Pat, thank you," Flora asked him to wait while she found her handbag and made sure the jewellery box was stored safely away, trying desperately to pull herself together.

Which is hard when you feel as though your world is falling apart around you.

FIFTEEN

Thankfully, they passed no one on their way down to the coach house, though as they were about to turn off the main driveway and onto the path to her little home, Flora and Pat heard both Frank and Reggie – who had gone on ahead – suddenly begin making enough noise to raise the dead.

"You wait here, I'll check it out," Pat said quickly.

Flora was about to say that she'd rather they stuck together, when there was a pause in Frank's barking long enough for Flora to hear Reggie squawking, "Tina the Terror!"

"I think it's just Betty," she said in relief, though Pat

was already strides ahead of her. When Flora arrived at the small clearing in front of her cottage, she was met by both Betty and Harry. Pat was chastising Frank, who had let himself be petted under the chin by Harry, hence his sudden quiet, and Betty was holding little Tina in her arms while Reggie flew circles above them all.

"You'd better come in," Flora's voice was the sound of pure resignation, and Pat raised his eyebrows at her in understanding – the last people they needed in the middle of the situation right now were their lovely elderly neighbours.

"Aye well, you can't have expected me to sit at home and do nothing when you ended our conversation like that!" Betty was indignant, "You must've known we'd come to check on you!"

Flora racked her brain to think of the conversation that Betty was referring to – so little time had passed since they had spoken, and yet so much seemed to have happened, "Sorry, Betty, it has been a… there's so much going on at the moment."

"Aye well, exactly why you need a cuppa and a natter. Get it all off your chest, like," Betty nodded her head decisively, her grey curls bobbing.

Clearly wondering why she had arrived home with the local policeman, Flora felt Harry's astute eyes watching her as she unlocked the front door. She knew that she would have to tell them something, maybe a watered-down version of the truth, if she were to satisfy the older couple's need for reassurance that everything was okay with her.

"I'll be getting on then, Flora," Pat said pointedly as she stepped back to allow her visitors to enter the place first.

"Thanks Pat, keep me posted," Flora whispered, praying that she could keep this visit short and sweet.

Short it was not.

By the time they were onto their second pot of Earl Grey, Flora was almost ready to be quite rude about it and simply ask her guests to leave. Perhaps feign a migraine or some other temporary malady. Reggie had been sitting on his perch, resorting to flicking seed husks at them since he had made swift work of his bowl of grapes. For once, Flora felt his frustration. Harry seemed to have realised some twenty minutes ago that Flora was not going to say anything more of note, and had even suggested to his wife that they make a move, but Betty was oblivious. Either that, or she just refused to give up with the little information they had.

Flora felt that she had been quite forthcoming on the subject of the wedding – explaining to the couple that she and Adam had decided to postpone it, and hoping they'd take her purported reasons as truth – that neither she nor Adam wanted all of the pomp and circumstance, that they would prefer a more private event. As a means to appease Betty that the wedding of the decade would not be taking place in the village, Flora assured her that she was the first to know, before either the wedding planners or the vicar. Her friend did seem somewhat mollified by this, and yet here she was now, still trying to tease more out of her as if she could tell that Flora had held back.

"But it's all organised," Betty said for at least the fourth time, "surely it's simpler to go ahead than to cancel it all? And waste all that money?"

"Flora's finances are not our affair, love…"

"Hush Harry, Flora and I are having a heart to heart!"

"Well, ah," Flora prepared to repeat her answer yet again, "it's our big day. Mine and Adam's. And it has to be what we both want. He's very busy at the moment…" Flora realised she was about to veer into risky territory and quickly clamped her mouth closed.

"If it's second thoughts about that monstrosi… that cake, then I could always get Jean to help me rustle up a more traditional…!"

"No! No, thank you Betty, so thoughtful but, ah, that's the least of it actually."

"Oh aye?" Betty cocked one eyebrow and Flora knew the older woman thought she'd finally scored the hit.

"I just mean in the sense of everything that's planned, the cake is just a small part," Flora was trying not to sound snappish. Trying and failing.

"You seem tired, Flora love," Harry set his teacup and saucer down gently and stood, though Betty made no move to follow.

"I am actually, haven't been sleeping well," Flora was so grateful to him that she could have kissed Harry in that moment. Either that or burst into tears.

"Well, I could stay and do some jobs for you while you rest, dusting, hoovering…" Betty offered.

"No!" Flora and Harry spoke in unison, causing Betty to tut loudly.

Eventually the older woman got up to join her husband and Flora walked them to the door, stopping to hug both before she unlocked it, and brushing the tiny seed shells from the shoulder of Harry's jacket.

"Thank you both for coming," Flora said, " I appreciate it, really I do, and you'll be the first to know when we rearrange the ceremony. It'll just be something much smaller this time, more in keeping with us. I'd be grateful if you could keep the news, ah, under your hat for the time being, though."

"We understand," Harry spoke for the couple, whilst Betty looked like she was chewing on a wasp.

To Flora's relief, however, her friend said nothing further to express her displeasure, simply picking up her little dog and following her husband out.

"Get out of it!" Reggie shouted after them, his hosting skills still sorely lacking.

"Reginald Parrot!"

"You're my honey! We're a team!" the little bird nuzzled into the crook of her neck, knowing full well that Flora couldn't stay mad at him for long.

Besides, she had much more pressing things to think about than her parrot's manners, Flora thought, as she rushed to her handbag to check her phone. Seeing that she had missed a call from Adam, Flora tried to stave off the wave of anger and anxiety that hit her. She should have had her phone out, listening. She should have got rid of her visitors quicker... round and round her mind whirred as she hit call back and listened to the dialling tone ringing out again.

Her face creased in consternation and frustration, Flora didn't hear the knock on the door until Reggie flew back down the hallway shouting, "Somebody else! Now there's trouble!"

"Be quiet, silly bird, I'm on the phone, and it'll be Betty. Look she's forgotten her silk scarf," Flora picked up the pretty item from the hallway radiator as she walked past and opened the door with one hand, her other still clutching the phone to her ear, though it had gone to voicemail now.

"Here you go," Flora held out the scarf automatically, though she was not met with the kindly eyes of her friend. Indeed, where Betty's face should be there was instead a very broad chest encased in a black tee-shirt. Flora's gaze followed the path up the tattooed neck and onto the inked face, a silent scream stuck in her throat, as she dropped her phone and heard it clatter on the tiles. Rooted to the spot, it was as if time stood still.

SIXTEEN

Of course, it was really only a matter of a couple of seconds before the little green bird on her shoulder sensed Flora's distress and flew at the man looming large in their doorway.

"Bad bird! Bad bird! There'll be hell to pay!" he shrieked, his wings flapping wildly about the would-be intruder's face.

Completely unflummoxed by the attack, Carl Bramble simply stepped forward, manhandling Flora out of the way and slamming the door behind himself, shutting Reggie outside in the process.

Flora held her hand to her mouth, wondering if she

was going to throw up or faint before the man even had a chance to assault her. Still her treacherous, useless legs refused to work. Not that there was much point now anyway, as there was only one entrance or exit to the place, and this hulking brute was blocking it.

"My Flora!" Reggie's desperate shrieks could be heard dimly through the wooden door and Flora wanted nothing more in that moment than to be outside with him, running off down the hill, shouting for help and being rescued. As it was, she could only hope that the little fella realised he needed to fly off and find help. And quickly, too.

"Flora, Flora Miller!" The man had his hands on her shoulders now, shaking her as if she had missed the first part of the conversation. Flora was forced to tune back in to him, though her mind wanted to stay outside with Reggie. His touch was surprisingly gentle, though, and as soon as he realised he had Flora's attention, Carl quickly removed his hands.

"Flora, take a deep breath, I'm not going to hurt you," his voice was so like Adam's that if Flora closed her eyes she could perhaps even believe it was her fiancé here with her, "I just need to talk to you, that's all, then I'll leave." The man ran his fingers over his well-marked, shaven scalp, as if his hair still remained, and the gesture was so familiar it brought a lump to Flora's throat.

"Just leave now, then," Flora's words came out in a breathy whisper, her body trembling with the force of trying to keep her fear at bay.

"I can't do that, Flora, let's sit down," he took her by the elbow with a gentleness that Flora wouldn't have believed such a man possessed, then steered her down the hallway to the sitting room, plonking them both down on the sofa.

"I'll scream, I'll scream for help," Flora threatened, rather belatedly, "Reggie is probably in the village now, getting the police here."

"Well, we both know that no one would hear you. And, ah, isn't that your bird at the window there?"

Sure enough, there was Reggie sitting on the outside window ledge staring back at them dolefully. His head was cocked to the side, as if he couldn't quite work out why there was a pane of glass between himself and the all-important seed bowl.

"Stupid bird," Flora muttered, then instantly regretted it. *What if she never saw him again? Never got to stroke his feathers. How would Adam live with it if his brother killed her after just killing his colleague and friend?*

"Flora!" his voice was harsher now, "You need to stay with me. We don't have long before they realise I'm in here."

"Exactly, exactly, Pat Hughes and Adam will be here any minute… with backup!"

"I didn't mean your hapless local bobby or my do-gooder brother," he sighed, long and loud, a sound of pure exasperation, "I'm talking about THEM."

"Who?" Flora wasn't sure she wanted to know, but as per usual she couldn't help herself. Curiosity would definitely kill the cat one of these days, she was sure of it. Hopefully it wouldn't be today.

"The gang. The Flames. They're already focused on this village, for more than one reason. If Adam thought he could keep you secret here, that ship sailed long ago!"

"No! It can't be! And they've sent you here to… to… and after you killed Blackett and all," she couldn't voice her fears, and even mentioning Blackett's name caused Flora to feel like she might vomit.

"I haven't killed anyone Flora, not since my release anyway, but yes, what I'm saying is true. More importantly, they don't know I'm in here with you right now, and they have no idea I'm done with them. I'm not doing another stint for him, I've done my time. He'll come after me, when he ties up the 'loose ends' here, but I'll take my chances. Adam's the only thing he can threaten me with now, that and my head on a plate, and I intend to preserve both. For the first time, I'm trying to do what's right. Help me here, please Flora! What did the shrink on the parole board say I was..? Reformed, that's me, you have to believe me."

Flora didn't believe him, but she played along. *What choice did she have?* "So, they think you're here in the village at their bidding and you're really here to…"

"Warn my brother. You need to get the message to him, Flora. He's next on their list. And you too if you interfere any more. That Russian bastar… Flora he won't give up. He's like a machine."

"I haven't interfered, I'm not even sure how or who…" Protesting was pointless, she knew, "And if I agree to tell Adam?"

"I'll leave you here and go and give them false intel – try to give you both as much time as possible to get away or for his colleagues on the force to do their jobs for once and catch them. The clock's ticking, though, Flora, do you understand? Tell me you understand what's at stake here."

"Get away?" Flora's mind missed his last questions as it began whirring with where she and Adam would go, who else she had unwittingly put in danger, and why she could hear Elvis lyrics again.

"Is that your bird singing?" Carl shot up from his seat and rushed to the window, being careful to hide behind the ample frilly curtain to the side.

"Yes, he's only recently picked it up…"

Carl ran from the room, "Time's up, Flora, heed my words, tell Adam!" And with that he rushed out of the front door, a small green bird appearing from the sitting room side of the cottage and flying hot on his heels as Carl charged around the opposite side of the building towards the back.

"Reggie! Reggie!" Flora screamed, the thread that was holding her emotions in check finally snapping.

Thankfully, the little ball of green came hurtling back at her words, and Flora slammed the door, bolted it, and then sat down on the cold floor amongst the wreckage of her mobile phone. She had no idea what to make of that conversation, only that she needed to speak to Adam. Fast. But without her phone she had no way to get hold of him.

"Think, think, think," Flora spoke aloud, inwardly cursing herself for letting the man in in the first place, for dropping her phone, for actually, well, sort of believing him.

"You think!" Reggie squawked back, thoroughly out of sorts and not understanding what on earth was going on. He perched on Flora's knee, lifting one foot and then the other in a sort of slow-motion, on the spot stomp.

Flora could feel his little claws through her linen trousers and the small pricks of pain helped keep her centred and focused on the present.

At length, a plan formulated in her mind. She couldn't risk leaving the house herself, that was certain, and for once Flora intended to do exactly what she thought Adam would tell her to do if he were here.

Lock the door. Hunker down. Wait for help.

Better late than never, she thought morosely.

"Right Reggie, it's all on you little chap," Flora whispered, knowing that her plan was silly at best and downright ridiculous at worse. Nevertheless, it was all she had to work with right now, "Have you ever fancied yourself as a carrier pigeon?"

SEVENTEEN

Flora didn't claim to know a lot about birds. Indeed, everything she had learnt had come from Reggie, whom she assumed was not typical even of his own breed! A quick search online helped her rule out her first idea, which was to find a container small enough to be portable but large enough to hold a tiny note, whilst also having a strap that could go over his little body. Double yellow headed parrots are much smaller than pigeons and so Flora had to concede that her companion would not be able to fly with such a contraption across his chest or back – and that was even if Flora could have cobbled one together from what was in her home.

The next concept involved medical tape from the first

aid box stored under the kitchen sink, and the small, pointed lid from a little tube of face blemish cream. Flora tried all ways to write a note tiny enough to fit in the equally tiny lid, and then eventually gave up, worried that sticking the tape to Reggie's leg would leave a sore patch when she eventually had to remove it.

Painfully aware that the clock was ticking, and glad that she'd never had a heartfelt ambition to be an inventor, Flora decided a quick snack, something to raise her blood sugar might help her think faster. Since she hadn't been in the tearoom to bring any leftovers home, this meant having the only thing available in her kitchen – a piece of the fruit she bought in for Reggie. Flora peeled the banana slowly, feeling the heat of her feathered friend's stare as he anticipated the treat to come. For herself, the nausea from earlier returned full force and Flora knew she wouldn't be able to stomach anything right now. She broke off the tip of the banana and gave it to Reggie, picking up the skin to throw in the bin.

And then her Eureka moment hit! Flora grabbed the pen she had been using for the paper notes and tore off a small strip of banana peel. She wrote briefly and to the point, HELP! AT COACH HOUSE and then debated whether to keep the strip flat or to roll it.

Reggie was becoming impatient for the rest of the treat now, and Flora knew she'd have to bribe him to complete the task. Certainly, she didn't want the bird hungry when she asked him to carry fruit rind in his mouth!

The second part of the plan relied on Tanya being back in the tearoom by now, and Flora had no control over that. She could only pray as she fed Reggie a fifth piece of banana, all the while whispering to him, "Welcome to the tearoom! Find Tanya! She's a corker!" on repeat.

"Tanya! She's a corker! Welcome to the tearoom!" Regie repeated between mouthfuls.

"It's now or never, little friend," Flora said as she gently popped the strip of banana peel horizontally in his little mouth, scooped Reggie up and then opened the window in the kitchen, "Go, quickly find Tanya! She's a corker! Tearoom!"

Gently propelling him forward, Flora hoped that the bird would understand his task, and wouldn't stop en route to the tearoom to try to eat his precious cargo. As she sent a silent prayer heavenward, Flora could do nothing but wait now to see whether her, admittedly rather outrageous, plan worked.

A remarkably short time later – Flora figured it was less than five minutes according to her wall clock in the kitchen, which had ticked every second through ominously as she waited – a little green ball flew back through the kitchen window, which had been left ajar. If she was thinking clearly, of course Flora would've locked it after her bold feathered friend set off on his important quest, but of course she was not. As it was, that worked out perfectly, as Reggie simply returned to his point of origin. To be honest, Flora felt a sense of despair and failure when she saw the bird return so quickly – sans the banana peel as well – presuming that he had been unable to complete his task. And that was assuming the little guy had even understood the requirements of the job in the first place. No, the disappointment Flora felt was all her own, and she scooped him from the window sill with both hands cupped and nuzzled the bundle of green against her nose.

"Good bird! My Flora!" Reggie chirped happily, quite full of himself, and eying the remaining banana on the counter.

"Well done, Reggie," Flora whispered, setting him down next to the chopped fruit and letting the bird take his fill.

"Flora! Flora! Are you there?" The sudden hammering coming from the front door caused Flora to jump and Reggie, with his mouth half full, to exclaim, "Get out of it!" in displeasure.

Remembering to check the all-important spy hole this time, Flora couldn't describe the relief she felt to see Tanya standing on the other side. Indeed, her swell of emotion was such that big, fat tears were rolling down Flora's face as she pulled the door open enough for her friend to enter and then locked it quickly behind her.

"Flora! What has happened? I got the shock of my life when your little bird arrived at the tearoom window without you... and then when I saw the strange little piece of fruit skin... goodness me! And you are crying? I hurried here as fast as I could, but I had to lock up and his wings are speedier than my legs," Tanya paused for breath and managed a hollow smile, but Flora could sense that her friend was also teetering on the brink of releasing a lot of pent up emotion.

Pulling away from her friend's tight embrace, Flora took a moment to look at Tanya properly. For the first time, well, ever, Tanya was not wearing her customary red lipstick, nor did she appear to have on make-up of any kind. Whilst it was usual for Flora herself to forgo the face paint most days, it was unheard of for her close friend. What had been a concern that she was still to act upon, now became an all-bells ringing, blaring warning in Flora's head.

First things first, though, she needed to call Adam on Tanya's mobile and ask him to hotfoot it over to Baker's Rise. Then she wasn't letting Tanya out of her sight until she'd spilled what was bothering her.

"Flora, love I got your message from earlier, I'm on my way to the village now, ten minutes I'll be there," there was no time for hellos or pleasantries of any kind as Adam spoke through the Bluetooth link in his car.

"I can't tell you how relieved that makes me, because he's been here, in the coach house!" Flora shrieked the last bit but couldn't help herself. All of her anxiety from earlier had returned full force.

"Carl? By God, Flora, is he gone? Has he hurt you?"

"Yes, Carl, yes he's gone and no he didn't hurt me. He asked me to pass a message to you… just get here fast."

"I'm putting my foot down, love, lock the door, don't leave."

"I know, I have Tanya here, see you soon," the line

went down and Flora slumped into her armchair in the sitting room, her head in her hands.

"Here," Tanya came through from the kitchen and handed her a cup of chamomile tea, "I couldn't help overhearing, is everything okay?"

"Yes, I, well as I said when you came in I dropped my mobile..."

"But why couldn't you leave the house and come to see me yourself?" Tanya asked gently, sitting on the sofa opposite.

The tears began again in earnest and Flora blew lightly on her cup watching the steam swirl. She knew that she wasn't at liberty to divulge any of the case, but nevertheless she owed her friend an answer, "There's been another murder... no one in the village... but it involves Adam directly and there are... some bad men looking for him. They can use me to get to him, so I have to stay hidden."

The crash of Tanya dropping her cup on the floor filled the small room, though broken china was the last thing on Flora's mind when she saw the distraught expression on her friend's face.

"Flora, I... I am to blame. It is all my fault."

EIGHTEEN

"How can it be your fault, Tanya?" Flora sounded snappier than she'd intended – to say she was confused was an understatement. Flora wondered if Tanya had understood her correctly when she'd tried to explain the situation. Normally her friend's English was excellent, but if the large, grey bags under her eyes were anything to go by then she hadn't been getting much sleep lately. *Perhaps Tanya was ill after all and was secretly going for medical appointments and treatment?* Flora felt awful that her friend may have been going through that alone.

Sensing the tension, and yet wanting to sleep on his perch with his tummy so full as it was, Reggie simply pulled his head out from where it had been hidden under a wing and squawked, "Secrets and lies! My Flora! Pipe down!"

"Yes, well, we'll have less of that, even if you are my little feathery hero!" Flora exclaimed in his direction, before turning her attention back to Tanya.

Moving to sit on the settee with her friend, Flora put her arm around Tanya's thin shoulders, feeling the quaking beneath her very demure, grey top. No neon or dinosaurs today.

"It is a long story," Tanya began slowly, "and not one I am proud of."

"Go on," Flora encouraged softly.

"Well, you know before I came to the village I lived in London, with Dmitriy, and that he was into... bad stuff."

"Yes, you told me that you ran away as you didn't want to be tangled up in all his criminal activities."

"Exactly, well, the past always comes back to haunt us, dear Flora, no matter how hard we try to shove our skeletons back in the cabinet."

"We all have a skeleton or three in our closet," Flora

whispered, "you met Gregory, right?"

"Ah yes, except mine comes with guns and threats," Tanya shook her head sadly, as if all the fight was suddenly gone from her body, while Flora's gasp could be clearly heard as she started to put two and two together. She just hoped she wasn't making five.

"Just so I'm clear," Flora began cautiously, "are you saying that Dmitriy is back in your life… and he's armed and threatening you?"

"Exactly that," Tanya's chin wobbled as she made the admission.

"But that's not your fault, Tanya, you have nothing to be guilty for. Why has he even sought you out after all this time? If he's worried about what you might know from before, then why now?"

"What? Oh, well apparently he found me shortly after I ran, but didn't see me as worth his effort to chase and bring back. I wasn't useful enough then. Wanted to bide his time – nobody betrays Dmitriy Morozov and gets away with it indefinitely, their time will always come – and for me that time is now, Flora. As for my guilt, well, a man like that always wants something, you know? Tries to persuade you that if you give it to him, he'll let you go and return to your new life."

"He wants you?" Flora was a bit confused.

"No, Flora!" Tanya herself was becoming more exasperated now, as if she simply didn't have the energy to explain, "He wants Adam! And you. Blackett he already has... ah, had."

"Oh my goodness!" Flora's hand flew to her throat as the full import of that statement sank in, "He has been threatening you so you'll give him inside information? On our whereabouts and... but why is he interested in us?"

"Has Adam told you about a gang called The Flames?"

"Ah, well..." it was pointless being ambiguous now, as Tanya seemed to know more than Flora herself did, so she ploughed on, "he has, his ah, well, he has a family member who is linked to the cartel, who told me that it's run by a Russian who... oh my! That's Dmitriy, isn't it? He runs the gang!"

"He's the boss, yes, or drug lord as he prefers to be called. I tried, Flora, I promise. I tried to pay him off with the only thing of enough value that I could get my hands on quickly, to get him to give up and turn his sights back south," Tanya paused and turned away, looking at Reggie and avoiding Flora's questioning gaze.

"With the emeralds from the manor house?" Flora let
the barely audible question hang between them, as a
charged silence followed. Hoping desperately that she
had simply jumped to assumptions.

At length, Tanya turned back to her, her eyes
glistening with unshed tears, "Yes, Flora, I stole from
you. I am so sorry. I believed it to be for your own
good, yours and Adam's, but that is no excuse. He took
the precious pieces and then still didn't call off his
dogs. You and Adam are in danger and, as I said, it is
all my fault."

Flora was just trying to process all of that when
another knocking started up out front and Reggie
awoke with extreme annoyance.

"Shut yer face! There'll be hell to pay!" his shrieks
followed her down the small hallway.

Flora took a deep breath in and released it slowly.

"Flora! It's me!" Even though she recognised Adam's
voice, knowing now how similar it was to his brother's
Flora checked the spy hole in the door to confirm it
was indeed her fiancé.

"Adam!" Rather embarrassingly, Flora flung herself
into his arms the moment the door was open wide

enough, "Tanya is here and… It's all a mess!" Flora sobbed into his chest as Adam walked them both into the house, one arm around Flora and the other reaching behind to lock the door.

"Aye, but it's not your mess, love, it's on me and the team to catch Blackett's killer."

"Not my mess?" Flora pulled back abruptly, the look on her face incredulous, "Not my mess! Goodness Adam, so far today I've had a bird accused of theft, which turned out to be my best friend. I've fainted on a man trying to propose, had a visit from your psychopath sibling, and now I've found out that Tanya's being threatened and blackmailed for information on you and me!" Flora's voice rose higher and higher until she stopped suddenly, realising her throat was hurting with the effort.

"Someone else was proposing to you?" Adam asked, his forehead scrunched tight and his eyes alarmed.

"That's your takeaway? Really, Adam?" Flora was angry now, and she couldn't seem to rein it in.

"Well, I love you and I've spent the whole drive over here berating myself for ever having chosen to leave your side since this whole tragic thing began, and now I can see with my own eyes that you're okay, but it doesn't sound as if everything is alright at all. I mean, I know it's not, but I thought all you'd have to do is lay low… Argh, can we start again, from the beginning? We'll sit down, you'll tell me everything, slowly… okay, love?"

Flora wasn't okay. Not okay at all. But she nodded and let him lead her into the sitting room, where Reggie had already returned to his perch, and currently had seeds stuck to his face. Obviously, another snack could solve all woes. Normally, Flora would be inclined to agree. But not today. Today, she couldn't stomach even the mention of food. She even skipped offering Adam a coffee, keen as she was to fill him in on everything. The poor man looked like he had been wearing the same clothes for days – had slept in them, if he'd even kipped at all – and Flora felt bad for him. And for Tanya. And even for herself. She wasn't sure if she could take any more and certainly didn't want to give a post-mortem of the day's events.

"I should go," Tanya said sombrely when she saw the two enter the room.

"No!" Flora commanded, her anger again getting the better of her. "No," she added more softly, "Adam will want to hear what you have to say, straight from the horse's mouth so to speak."

Tanya really didn't look happy with that idea, but she stayed sitting where she was, as Flora took a seat beside her and Adam perched on the armchair, leaning forwards intently, his hands steepled above elbows which rested on his knees.

"So ladies," he began as if back in the interrogation room, all hint of the emotion from the hallway gone from his voice, "let's start at the beginning of the day."

NINETEEN

When more tears had been shed, and her heart-breaking confessions repeated, Tanya left to go home. There was little point in re-opening the tearoom now so late in the afternoon. Adam had advised her to confide in Pat, and for the two of them to stay safe together. He had offered to pull some strings and have them taken to a safe house, but Tanya had dismissed the idea out of hand, determined as she was to not have her life stolen from her by Dmitriy for a second time.

Now that he knew the leader of The Flames had his sights set on Baker's Rise, the detective immediately contacted his Chief Superintendent to have more resources allotted to the village.

"I'll be staying with Flora till the immediate danger is neutralised," Flora heard Adam saying, from where she was standing in the kitchen, leaning out into the hallway and towards the sitting room door to have a really good stretch. Not eavesdropping at all.

"Adam," Flora began when his call ended and she handed him the coffee she'd just made, "you don't need to babysit me, really."

"I've lost Blackett, I'm not losing you as well!" Adam said, rather more forcefully than he'd intended, "Besides, you've had my brother barge his way into your own home just this afternoon, surely you'll be happier having me here?"

"I'm always happier having you here," Flora began slowly, "but you haven't given me a chance to explain about Carl yet. You were straight on the phone after Tanya left."

"Aye well, I can imagine it was more of his usual. More bullying threats, more frightening women to get the information he wants."

"Actually, no," Flora said matter-of-factly, surprised when her heart didn't start up with palpitations again just thinking about the man's visit.

"No?" Adam was incredulous, "You mean he's broken the habit of a lifetime?" His sneer was not an attractive look.

Flora took a deep breath and explained what Carl had said and how he had actually come to warn them.

"I just don't believe it," Adam shook his head forcefully, "It'll be another tactic, a ploy to gain your trust. And that's one thing you must never do, Flora, is to trust my brother."

"He seemed so genuine, so sincere," Flora muttered, though she was starting to doubt her own recollections now.

"He's had a lot of practice," Adam scoffed.

"Well, either way, between what he told me and what we know from Tanya, it seems it wasn't just Blackett on the gang's hit list," Flora was sick to her stomach of the whole conversation to be honest and she stood and moved over to look out of the window.

Alerted by her movement, Reggie flew from his perch to her shoulder and chirped, "My Flora, silly old bird," as he waddled up and down.

"Maybe I am silly," Flora whispered back, not intending Adam to hear. As it was, he must have come up behind her quietly, and now slid his arms around her waist.

"You're not silly at all love," he whispered right beside the shell of her ear, "this is the stuff of cop shows, not sleepy English villages. It's a lot to take in. You always like to think the best of people, and I love that about you, but some folk... well there's no good left in them."

Flora turned in his arms and saw the stark sadness in her fiancé's eyes. Kissing him gently on the cheek, Flora felt Adam sag against her, as he finally allowed some of the tension from recent events to leave his body, his forehead coming to rest on hers.

Moments passed in silence until, as if to change the subject, Adam asked, "Did you speak to the Crawfords and cancel the wedding?"

Moving them both to the sofa, Flora sighed as she replied, "No, I saw Tammy, but, ah, there wasn't the opportunity to explain or to cancel anything. She was rather upset about the way things panned out the other day, and seeing her ex-fiancé so unexpectedly. She wanted me to ask you for his contact number, or for us to get a message to him. She was very upset, as you can imagine."

"You didn't tell her he was... ah passed, did you?" Adam's eyes were cool again and his jaw set in a firm line.

"Well, I... yes, actually, I had little choice."

"You could've just said no!"

"Well, I didn't feel that I could actually."

"You're too nice, Flora," Adam's voice softened then and he ran his hands through his hair agitatedly.

"Surely you must have recognised her, the few wedding planning appointments you came to?" Flora asked, her own anger rising again now, and a sense of deep fatigue settling into her bones, "It can't all be on me. If you'd warned me, then perhaps we could have avoided them encountering one another."

"Well, for one, I didn't know he was coming up to the big house that day, and for two, I had never actually met her before then."

"Really?" It was Flora's turn to sound incredulous.

"Really. He is... ah was, a very private man. He insisted on keeping his work and personal life very separate. Something I'm only now beginning to appreciate," Adam said, rather too sardonically for Flora's liking, "He told me when they got engaged, and then mentioned they had split up later, a few months after the fact, when I asked after her. Irreconcilable differences, apparently."

"Well there was only really one main point of contention between them from what Tammy told me, and that was her father and his shady accounts. You don't think he could've..?"

"Pah! No, it was definitely a professional job. Not just some bumbling ex father in law with a grudge to settle."

Flora couldn't bear the almost mocking tone in Adam's voice any longer. That he was swinging hot and cold she understood, of course, as she herself was guilty of that too. But the idea of them being trapped in this little cottage together while they were both feeling this way? Well, it might well tear them apart.

"So, what's the plan?" Flora asked, after an uncomfortable silence.

"The plan is that we find somewhere to stay for a few days until some progress is made on the case."

"That could be weeks, though, couldn't it?" Flora's

stomach sank at the thought of having another prolonged stay with Betty and Harry, as much as she had been happy to help her friends when Harry had pneumonia. Thankfully she quickly concluded that they didn't have enough room to host both her and Adam anyway.

"It could, but I'm hoping some new intel will come in as to Car… ah, the killer's whereabouts. Blackett had been working on some gang-related murders off and on for a while, so the team aren't starting from scratch. They even have hopes that they've managed to place someone undercover on the inside."

"Carl said he didn't kill Blackett."

"What?"

"Just that. He said it wasn't him. I'm not sure I believed him at the time, and I'm even less sure now, but there you have it. That was what he said. I guess it must've been Dmitriy then."

"No, he never gets his own hands dirty, always gets his minions to do it for him. Except with his women, of course, he enjoys making them suffer."

"Of course. Poor Tanya…" Flora felt the tears about to overwhelm her again and took a moment to count to ten in her head, "so, who is the murderer then?"

"My bet's still on my own flesh and blood," Adam said bitterly, standing and moving abruptly to the hallway when his phone started to ring.

At the same moment, there was a sharp rap on the front door, and Flora found herself frozen to the spot.

Perhaps we aren't going to need alternative accommodation after all, she thought, rather dramatically, *perhaps this is the end of the road for us both.*

TWENTY

"If they were going to get a sniper to murder us both in this coach house, they would do it through a window and not through the spy hole in the front door," Adam whispered whilst he and Flora were in the kitchen preparing a pot of Earl Grey for their guest.

He was referring to Flora – who had finally found the impetus to rush from the sitting room – having jumped on her fiancé's back, piggyback style, to halt his progress when he moved to check who was standing on the front step.

"Yes, well," Flora snapped back in a stage whisper, rubbing her own back which was protesting from the unusual activity, "you wouldn't be saying that if you were dead!" Ignoring the ridiculousness of her own statement, Flora swept past her fiancé carrying the large teapot and three cups on a tray.

Reggie, who was at his limit for visitors for the day, had had to be temporarily shut in the bedroom, as calling the vicar's wife an "old trout" and a "fetid fart" was definitely deemed unacceptable by polite society.

"So, Sally, I'm so sorry it completely slipped my mind that you were coming round," Flora apologised again, when the usual pleasantries such as the weather had been rushed through, accompanied as they were by Reggie's angry squawks from the neighbouring room of "There'll be hell to pay!" which had now thankfully changed to a more plaintiff, "We're a team!"

As he had no doubt intended, it did tug on Flora's heart strings for a moment, until the silly bird rallied with another round of "Stupid jerk!" and she tried once more to tune him out.

"Well, I'm sorry to bother you, I know you're so busy at the moment with the wedding…" Flora was about to interrupt Sally then, to tell her what she had been phoning to discuss that morning – that the preparations had been halted – but the vicar's wife continued without pausing for breath, "but Shona came to have a word with me at the vicarage this afternoon, and now I urgently need to discuss next month's summer fete with you."

"The summer fete?" The question was merely a squeak as it dawned on Flora that she had completely forgotten one of her main annual responsibilities as the lady of the manor – organising the fayre in its entirety.

"I'll leave you two ladies to it," Adam said, excusing himself to return to the kitchen, and in doing so leaving Flora to deal with it alone. Not that it was anyone's responsibility but her own...

"Yes," Sally continued, setting her cup down on the coffee table and fiddling with the gold cross pendant she always wore at her neck, "given the events of last year, the showdown in the beer tent between her father and his ex-wife, and then his tragic death, Shona understandably doesn't want to put up a tent this year. She would prefer to avoid the event entirely, as would her fiancé, Will. Although I hate to admit it, that drinking station is normally rather a focal point of the whole show and we do rely on the local vet to judge the animal competitions..." Sally trailed off, looking at Flora expectantly, if not for a solution then at least for some words of wisdom.

Flora had neither. Her mouth hung open like one of the goldfish that people used to win at fairs in days gone by, and she struggled to form even one coherent thought on the subject. Oh, of blackmail, of murder and coercion, she had many thoughts, but on this subject? Nada. It just didn't seem so important in the grand scheme of things.

The silence drew out, punctuated only by the hum of Adam's low voice in the background as he spoke to his colleagues, and by Reggie's – thankfully now only occasional – outbursts. Both women reached for their cups of tea at the same moment, looked up and caught each other's eye, and then smiled.

"I'm sorry," Sally said, "for dropping this on you. I feel like I've walked in on something important. Is everything okay?" Her bright hazel eyes always showed compassion, never judgement, and Flora could sorely do with an impartial confidante right about now.

"Well," Flora spoke slowly, choosing her words carefully so that she didn't accidentally divulge information which was another's story to tell, "Adam's colleague has been murdered. Detective Blackett, who you will have spoken to in past investigations."

"Oh my goodness," Sally raised a hand to her chest in shock, "may the poor man rest in peace with our Lord Jesus."

"Yes," Flora tried to fight back the tears, but just the relief of opening up to her friend, even in some partial manner, was trigger enough to set the waterworks going again, "sorry, I, ah…"

"Not at all, if must have been such a shock for you both."

"It was, and ah, it seems he may not have been the only target."

"Oh no. They are after Adam as well." It may have been her years as a vicar's wife, or before that as a teacher, but Sally had a way of understanding what was unsaid. Of reading between the lines without you needing to explain in words. For this, Flora was very grateful.

"Yes, and me too perhaps. It's an established gang, and ah, Adam has some personal ties, that is, another invested reason in finding the culprit if you see what I mean…" Flora knew she was being rather cryptic, but she didn't dare speak more clearly. The fewer people who had all the details the safer it would be.

"Hmm, I think I see," Sally spoke slowly, and then more resolutely, "So, Flora, what can James and I do? What help do you need?" She stood up and came over to hug Flora, rubbing her shoulder gently.

"Oh, nothing, just letting me offload a bit is... well, I'm so grateful."

"Of course, but," Sally had resumed her seat on the sofa and was looking thoughtful, "look, if Adam isn't going back to Morpeth tonight – I'm guessing he won't want to leave you alone? So, why don't you both come to stay at the vicarage? We have a couple of spare rooms, and if you can put up with three excited girls, who chatter non-stop and will want to style your hair and paint your nails, then you'd both be very welcome!"

"Really?" Flora sniffed loudly and dabbed at her eyes and nose, wondering how her friend could have known exactly what it was she needed, "we could certainly do with a bit of a refuge, truth be told. We aren't very, ah, well, safe here."

"Then it's settled. I'll head back and make up the beds, and then you two will come along later? Oh, and Reggie too?"

"Oh, I hadn't thought, but yes, sorry, will it be okay to bring him?"

"Of course, you will absolutely make my girls' day, their week even!"

"Thank you so much," Flora felt some of the tight ball of knots in her stomach unravel slightly, and that she could finally take a full, deep breath again, "thank you, Sally, you have no idea how grateful I am."

"Not at all, a friend in need and all that… besides, I'm always looking for extra hands with the childcare!" She winked, putting Flora even more at ease with the plan, and allowing her for this brief moment to think that perhaps everything might work out okay after all.

TWENTY-ONE

"Miss Flora!" The shrill shouts of three little voices were amplified in the small dining room at the vicarage and Reggie, who had a makeshift perch on the window sill, puffed out his little chest feathers, as of course he must be the cause of the girls' evident happiness.

"Welcome to the tearoom!" He said proudly, though even he did a quick scan of the strange room, followed by a sharp shake of his head as if for a moment wondering where on earth he was.

It had been after dark when Flora and Adam had arrived the night before, with Reggie in his little carrier refusing to accept the journey quietly despite the late hour. The Marshall girls had already been tucked up in bed, and Sally and James had welcomed the couple warmly, with a quick nightcap and words of reassurance. Surprising herself, Flora had managed to sleep deeply for the first time that week, and woke up feeling somewhat refreshed. Looking at Adam now across the breakfast table, she thought that he too appeared slightly less washed out and jumpy than the day before.

"Girls, let Flora and Adam eat in peace," Sally chided, but little Megan had already squeezed herself onto Flora's knee while Evie was bombarding her with questions about the Reggie stories. The quieter sibling, Charlotte, had gone over to stroke Reggie.

"Why you here?" Megan asked, sticking her thumb in her mouth, her eyes wide and wondering.

"Oh, ah… we thought… ah…" Flora didn't have much experience of answering children's questions honestly whilst also being vague enough to protect them from the truth.

Thankfully, Sally jumped in to save her, "There's a little problem at the coach house, so they came for a sleepover till it's sorted!"

"Boiler gone off?" Evie said very sagely, no doubt

remembering their previous problems with the old church hall heating system.

Flora nodded and smiled, and Sally didn't answer, simply letting the girl make her own assumptions.

"Oh, you'll have to see my new toys!" Evie had already moved onto another subject, in the lightning quick way that young ones do, and Flora's brim-full head could barely keep up.

"It was her birthday a couple of weeks ago," Sally explained.

"Yes, I have new cuddly wabbit!" Megan contributed, squirming to get down, no doubt to find the bunny in question.

"Do you have something to show me, Charlotte?" Flora asked, when the other two sisters had run off to gather their treasures for her perusal.

"I, um, yes, I have a new dolly," Charlotte blushed a deep red and then turned back to Reggie, burying her face in his head feathers.

"We have a tradition that each of the other two siblings gets one present for their sister's birthday," Sally explained.

"That's so lovely," Flora replied, having to swallow down a lump in her throat with no real understanding of why it was there.

"Shall we go through to the sitting room and talk things over?" James suggested, setting his coffee cup back down on the table gently.

For a member of the clergy, he was a man of very few words, Flora had noticed. Though, she did wonder if that was partly due to living in a house with four females! Poor man probably struggled to get a word in edgewise!

Sally had filled her husband in on the bare bones of the situation, as much as she knew of it, and as they all took a seat in the cheery front room it was James who spoke first.

"I'm so very sorry for the loss of your friend and colleague, Adam," he began, "I can only imagine how devastating it must be, especially since he was due to serve as your best man in just a few short weeks. I am guessing the wedding will be postponed for you to attend his funeral, and ah, do the policing involved in finding his killer?"

And just like that another weight was taken from Flora's shoulders. It made sense to postpone their wedding plans. It was clear as day to others. No big explanations needed. She smiled at Adam, who sat next to her on the old settee, and he returned the sentiment.

"Ah exactly," Adam replied, "It is of course deeply disappointing, but unavoidable."

"Absolutely," the vicar agreed gently, "I will mention it from the pulpit on Sunday, tell the whole congregation at once, so you don't have the discomfort of telling everyone individually."

"That is so kind," Flora whispered, "thank you."

"We've also been talking together about the annual summer fete," Sally began, nodding at her husband and smiling, as if what were to follow may have been his idea, "and we thought that perhaps we would miss it this year."

"Miss it as in you two not attend as well?" Flora asked, somewhat horrified.

"No, no, sorry I didn't explain myself very well, I meant, let's not have a summer fayre next month. Let's do something different this year, maybe an autumn celebration or… well, I'm sure the ladies of the W.I. will have plenty of suggestions… once they've expressed their displeasure of course!"

"I'm pretty sure they won't take the changing of a longstanding village tradition very well," Flora fretted.

"Definitely not, but times change, life happens and things crop up unexpectedly," Sally reassured her.

"Okay then, it sounds like a great plan. To be honest, I think my head will be in a better place in October," Flora felt herself smiling, another worry lifted, just like that.

"We were thinking maybe a harvest type of event, up at the farm," the vicar added, "with pumpkins and jam. I love a bit of fresh jam, you know!"

"It's his guilty pleasure," Sally added wryly, flashing a look of adoration at her husband, "and let's all pitch in with the organising. It's silly that it's always been left up to the family at The Rise. I mean, I've been told that Harold Baker persuaded his latest paramour to act as an event organiser every year, didn't lift a finger himself, and yet here you are, expected to do the lot. No. It's a village event, I'll make sure the village organises it."

"I'm not sure what to say, I… thank you," Flora fiddled with her summer dress, feeling like she really wasn't doing a very good job of this whole estate ownership thing.

"Don't be silly," James answered, leaning forward and catching Flora's eye, his expression earnest, "I will also announce this at church on Sunday. I'll simply cite a bereavement to explain both postponements. Nothing at all for you to apologise for. Now, I want you to know, you can both stay here for as long as you need until the situation is... resolved."

"I'm not sure how long that will be," Adam's gruff voice made Flora's heart ache, "I can't hide out indefinitely."

"Well, for a few days at least," James nodded as if that was decided and then rose, "now, I'm afraid I have a sermon to write, and if those elephantine stomps coming down the stairs are anything to go by, you have a morning of playing awaiting you!"

TWENTY-TWO

Flora shifted uncomfortably on the sofa, as she tried to discreetly remove some of the dozens of little plastic clips and bobbles which had been placed in her hair and which were now pulling uncomfortably. She was trying to catch Adam's eye, but he was staring absently out of the window, hardly even aware that his fingernails were now a fetching shade of fuchsia.

"And this is beach Barbie and this a Tinkerbell fairy from the film…" little Evie trailed on and on, oblivious to Flora's growing distraction.

"Adam," she whispered eventually, when the girls had finally become bored and had taken Reggie on a tour of the old house, "Adam!"

"Huh? Sorry love, miles away."

"It's okay, it's just that when Sally mentioned Harold using an events organiser it reminded me of the Crawfords. They were due at the manor house this afternoon to go over final choices and arrangements. Shall I just call them and explain it's all off? I mean, I'm pretty sure we won't get our deposits back, and some things we've already paid in full like the cake, but they'll need to cancel the marquee and the caterers and… well, I mean the money is the least of our worries, I know, and… " Flora stopped mid-sentence, trying hard to hide the wobble in her voice.

"Yes, love, best get it done now, eh?"

"No time like the present," Flora agreed, though just as she was taking her new-to-her phone from her bag – thankfully the vicar had a work mobile and a personal one and had been kind enough to let her use the latter until she could buy a new phone, her SIM card luckily having escaped the previous day's accident unscathed – the device started ringing of its own accord, "It's just Laurie," Flora told her fiancé as she answered the call and walked over to the large bay window.

"A break-in?... What do you mean? Like a sleeping bag or..? Okay, I'll call Pat," Flora ended the call, her mind whirring and the sick feeling in her stomach having returned to make her once again feel like curling up in a ball and hiding under the table.

Of course, Adam had heard her side of the conversation and was already on the phone to the local policeman, asking him to meet them him at the manor house.

"Call Laurie back," he said brusquely when he finished his conversation and turned back to Flora, "tell him to leave the house immediately and to make his way back to the village. It's too dangerous for him up there right now."

"Oh!" It was a pitiful sound, barely even a clear word, as Flora brought a shaking hand up to her mouth.

"Hey now, love," Adam had his arms around her in an instant, "I'm sure it's nothing. You wait here and I'll pop up there and clear it all up. Probably just local teenagers or a hiker who got caught short," he didn't sound like he was even convincing himself, let alone her, and Flora shook her head jerkily.

"No! Laurie says he's not sure if someone actually slept there, or just stashed their gear, but there's glass over the back patio from where they've smashed their way in. Where you go, I go right now. The property is my responsibility and we'll check it over together."

Adam opened his mouth as if to argue, then seemingly thought better of it and simply guided Flora from the room by her elbow, "Let's tell Sally and make this quick."

Sure enough, one of the panels in the big kitchen window had been smashed and then the sliding chain and heavy bolt on the back door apparently opened from the inside, perhaps to let the intruder come and go without having to climb through the window, or maybe even to let in his accomplices. Flora knew how this worked enough to figure that much out for herself, she didn't need Adam to explain it to her.

"Looks like a professional job, this," Adam muttered to himself as he examined the clear lines of the broken glass and then the way the key lock on the back door had been picked, "Perhaps you should stay in the car, love, go on back now. And take the bird with you." Flora could understand Adam's exasperated tone where Reggie was concerned, as unfortunately the little bird had got wind of her trying to sneak out of the vicarage without him, and had then clung to Flora's shoulder protectively, digging his claws in rather painfully and refusing to let anyone peel him off. Pressed for time as they were, Adam had eventually conceded that the parrot would have to come with them. The pair had eyed each other distastefully for the whole journey, with Reggie giving the detective his best side-eye from the comfort of Flora's shoulder, a distinct look of 'I've won' about him.

"No. We stay together. Isn't that what you always say? That I'm safer with you?"

"Well not always... but okay, let's be quiet now," he tapped Reggie's beak decisively, and the bird spread his wings to their full width and flapped them in Adam's face in protest.

They tiptoed through to the study, where Laurie had told her he'd found some cigarette butts beside her little sofa, and a tattered, army-style backpack hidden squashed behind the desk. Adam did a full sweep of the study, even asking Flora to open the secret room on the off chance that whoever it was had inadvertently managed to open the sliding door, but all was empty and they shut the hidden place up securely again. When they had done a similar search in all the other rooms of the house and landed back where they began, Flora finally let out the breath that felt like it had been squeezing her chest in a vice the whole time.

"I'll go and put the kettle on while we wait for Pat and Frank," Flora said, turning back to the doorway. Her feet froze on the spot and her breath hitched in her chest.

"Best make that a pot for three then, sweetheart," Carl said, his cocky grin sending shivers down Flora's spine.

TWENTY-THREE

"Lovely nails, brother, very pretty," Carl's voice was full of sarcastic humour, which matched his expression as he looked Adam up and down for the first time in well over a decade, "and thank you, Flora, for putting me up in your fancy house."

"Flora, could you make the tea please, love?" Adam gave her a pointed look and Flora hoped she had interpreted it correctly as she turned back to the man blocking the doorway. Carl stepped to the side and indicated she should pass with a gentlemanly flourish of his right arm, at which Flora scuttled past, hoping Reggie would follow her. So far, her little bird had been eyeing the tense reunion from his perch near the window, distracted by having found his seed bowl full on their arrival.

Unwilling to leave Adam alone, but also believing that he would want her to call McArthur and ask for backup, Flora rushed into the bright kitchen. The summer sun was shining through the wide windows, including the one missing its pane, as if it were a normal, beautiful day with none of the dark undertones that Flora knew were being discussed in the room next door. The arguing that she could hear coming through the dividing wall told her that she should hurry. Flora blinked twice against the sudden glare, coming as she did from the much darker hallway, and fumbled in her bag for her phone. Seeing that the kettle beside her was already half-filled, she clicked it on to boil as she pulled her mobile out.

"When no one else can understand me..." Reggie piped up from behind her, as Flora found the detective's number in her electronic address book and hit dial.

"Hush, silly bird," Flora chastised, without turning to look at the parrot who she assumed was perched on the top of the kitchen door, from where he usually liked to survey his empire.

"When everything I do is wrong..."

"I told you, this is import..." the words died on Flora's lips as she turned in the direction of the bird's voice, coming face to face with a man she recognised who was standing in the corner behind her, hidden from view by the kitchen door as she'd entered the room.

"Oh! Vic!" Flora exclaimed, as McArthur's phone went to voicemail, "I'm afraid I haven't been back in the bookshop yet..."

Instead of responding verbally, the man simply gave her a toothy grin, and she noticed for the first time the gold plating he had on a couple of his incisors, glinting in the strong sunlight. This wasn't Vic's normal, deferential demeanour, however, and the man stalked towards her suddenly as if Flora was very much prey to his predatory moves.

"You give me hope and consolation..." Reggie carried on regardless, and the repeated Elvis lyrics finally triggered something in Flora's brain. A memory that not only did he sing them whenever he saw the carpet fitter – a job which Flora was only now suspecting might well have been a ruse – but that he had also started up when they were at the coach house during Carl's visit there. As she recalled, at that time Adam's brother had rushed to the window, seen something – or rather someone – who had freaked him, and he had legged it.

It was starting to make sense now. What Carl had said about the gang having infiltrated her life even before Blackett's death and why this specific man had shown a particular interest in chatting to her, using a shared love of books as a cover.

I bet he can't even read, Flora thought rather unkindly, but she considered justified in her current predicament.

"You give me strength to carry on!" Reggie shrieked the last line of his current rendition and shot across the room to land on Vic's head.

"Ah!" the man shouted, shocked since all of his attention had been focused on moving towards Flora. The kettle bubbled loudly on the counter and the switch flicked off, all happening in the briefest of moments. Grabbing the kettle, and deciding that she needed to know for certain if the man in front of her was a member of The Flames, Flora jerked forwards and deliberately splashed some of the scalding material on his chest. Now, had she been thinking more clearly, she would have perhaps followed through on the action more thoroughly. But it was not in Flora's nature to hurt someone deliberately, and so she splashed him with only the smallest amount, enough to make the man rip off the expensive polo shirt he was wearing, his shout of pain filling the room.

"You bitch!" he exclaimed, his Slavic accent suddenly thick, and launching for Flora despite the burn making his moves sloppy.

Quick-footing it to the side, Flora darted behind him and saw what, deep down, she knew would be there – the large tattoo of a flame on the man's shoulder blade. Too late, her eyes travelled down his back, and she saw the gun that was tucked into the band of his designer jeans, just as Vic spun around with one hand going for the weapon and the other grabbing Flora and hauling her tightly against his naked, wiry torso.

Alerted either by the noise, or the little bird who Flora suddenly realised was missing from the scene, both Bramble brothers came barraging into the kitchen at that moment, Reggie hot on their heels.

"Not that jerk!" the parrot shrieked, as if trying to tell the men that Vic was the one he felt unsure of, the one he wanted away from his Flora.

"Vic," Carl breathed the word out as a warning, shaking his head slowly, as the man in question brought his hand up to hold the gun to Flora's temple. Her heart beat wildly in her chest as her captor's grip around her torso tightened, and Flora stared with wide, unblinking eyes at her fiancé.

Whichever way this went now, she knew it couldn't end well.

"Put the gun down," Adam said slowly, advancing one more step towards them.

"He's in the gang," Flora blurted out, then regretted it as Vic hissed in her ear, his grim breath making her stomach heave.

"One more word, bitch...! And you, one more step and she gets it!"

"Hush, love, I can see, don't worry, we've got you," Adam smiled, a weak attempt but a good try given their circumstances, "Carl, tell me who this little weasel is."

"Viktor Petrov, Dmitriy's second in command, and the man who actually killed your colleague." Carl was a big man, taller and broader that Adam, who himself was not small by any standards, yet Flora could sense that Vik was not cowed by the man's physical presence in the way most men would be. Coming from the underworld as he did, she supposed the inked scalp and face had no effect either.

Why her brain went on its own little detours in these situations, Flora didn't know. Perhaps it was to protect her mind from the real horror, the real desperation of the situation. Anyway, she tried hard to focus now, as Adam was speaking again.

"It's me the boss wants, Viktor, swap me for the woman and we'll leave together," Adam offered, looking Vik directly in the eye, his gaze not wavering at all.

"No!" Flora shrieked, earning her a harsh glare from both her fiancé and his brother. *Really, the similarity between their mannerisms was uncanny.*

"No need to go anywhere for that," Vik replied suddenly, slackening his hold on Flora in that instant and turning the gun to face Adam.

"No!" Flora shrieked again, as the sound of the weapon being fired brought a temporary deafness. Her legs finally gave out underneath her, but Flora clung to the counter for support, life seeming to have gone into slow motion, "Not Adam!"

TWENTY-FOUR

One moment he was standing to the side of his brother, the next Carl had flung himself in the path of the incoming bullet and taken the hit, square on the left of his large chest, dropping him like a sack of potatoes on the floor.

"Carl, no!" Flora heard Adam's cry as if through a haze of smoke or fog. She was aware of her fiancé launching himself forward and, desperate to avoid their assailant pulling the trigger for a second time, Flora grabbed the nearest thing to her, which happened to be the kettle. She swung her arm and hit Vik on the side of his face with the improvised weapon, giving Adam enough time to then wrench the gun free from the Russian's hand and grapple the man to the ground. That she could have poured the still-hot water over his head, didn't occur to Flora in her only semi-lucid state. Never mind, the metal jug had served its purpose, and Flora sank to her knees, feeling the softness of little feathers as a familiar weight landed on her shoulder and snuggled into the crook of her neck.

"What the heck is going on here?" Pat Hughes' shocked voice penetrated Flora's befuddled mind and she looked up to see the local policeman rushing in to take over from Adam, who was pressing one knee in to Vik's back. The killer's arms were also restrained behind him, effectively pinning his body to the ground.

"No, I've got him! My brother!" Adam shouted to Pat, directing the man's attention to the body lying lifeless on the kitchen floor. One look, and Flora's head knew what her heart would take longer to accept – Carl was gone.

As Pat felt for a pulse, and Adam watched on, the desperate hope in her fiancé's glistening eyes was what finally broke through Flora's fear and shock and made her launch her reluctant body forward. Crawling on her knees to the body, Flora tried to help by pressing her hands to the bloody wound.

"It's no good lass, he's gone," Pat whispered, the sympathy heavy in his voice.

"I should have helped him sooner, while Adam was…" Flora began.

"No, lass, no, looks straight through the heart to me. I'd say he died instantly, nothing either of you could do."

Pat took over from Adam, who reported the murder and the way his sibling had given his life to save him, his voice devoid of emotion. Flora knew it would hit him later, the reality of it seeping in as the shock wore off. She knew he would rerun the moments in his head on repeat, wondering what he could have done differently. She knew she would need to be strong for them both as he tried to come to terms with the wasted years and the loss of what could have been.

Her thoughts were interrupted by Tanya, who seemed to appear suddenly and helped Flora from the floor and into her embrace, "I didn't realise you were here too," Flora whispered, only now becoming fully aware of her surroundings again.

"Pat wouldn't leave me at the cottage, insisted I come up here with him, doesn't want to let me out of his sight now I took your advice and told him the truth, but it took us too long to get here. I'm so sorry," Tanya held Flora tightly to her, and both women were crying salty tears of grief and regret.

"Not your fault," Flora whispered, "just all so awful."

And it really was awful.

McArthur arrived shortly after with a crew of cars following, all of their blues flashing and the howl of sirens once again waking the sleepy village. She brought with her a detective whom Flora didn't recognise, but who seemed to have superiority in the force, as both she and Adam referred to him simply as 'Sir'. *Perhaps he was CID or something?* Flora didn't really know how these things worked, though there did seem to be a lot of non-uniformed operatives in her house all of a sudden, along with the usual officers that she had seen at too many murder investigations now.

Flora sat in the sitting room with Tanya, sharing a pot of Earl Grey that her friend had kindly made by boiling water in a pan on the hob, the kettle apparently having been removed as evidence. As Flora stood at the front window, watching Vik being escorted to a police van that was parked on the gravel forecourt, she saw the Crawfords pull up in their ancient Volvo, only to be turned away by the uniformed officer stationed at the top of the driveway. *Well the wedding was the least of her concerns now*, she mused, and Flora pushed all thought of it to the back of her mind.

Of course, there were questions. So many questions. Reggie had been collected by Sally, who had been handed the angry bundle of feathers by another officer before she could get anywhere near the front door. Apparently his shrieking cuss words and swooping on the detectives and investigators when they least expected it was not conducive to sweeping a crime scene and gathering evidence. Flora had been given no choice in the matter, and her sobs had renewed with full vigour when she had caught sight of the exchange from the window. *Pat must've called the vicar's wife,* she mused, not that she knew for certain. She and Tanya had been closeted away in here for what felt like hours, only being disturbed when another strange face came to ask her to go over the story for the umpteenth time.

Flora could only imagine how Adam was feeling. *Surely,* she thought, *they cannot be making him work the case?*

Eventually, Pat came in to collect Tanya, and said that they were being allowed home, but given how angry everyone assumed Dmitriy would now be, they would be escorted by two officers who would be stationed at the police cottage until further notice. This news caused Tanya's face to pale and her eyes to seek her husband's, their expression pleading.

"Please Patrick," she whispered, "When will this be over? Cannot Viktor tell where his boss is hiding out?"

"I know love, it's worrying and frustrating, but you are safe with Frank and me, come on now."

After hugging Flora and kissing her cheek, Tanya left the room without further comment, and Flora was left alone.

No Adam. No Reggie.

Just her thoughts and regrets, and of those she had plenty.

TWENTY-FIVE

Three days had passed since the murder at the mansion house. Adam had been given leave from work to grieve his brother's death and to make the final arrangements, and thankfully he had chosen to stay with Flora while he did so. They had hunkered down in the coach house, the tearoom and bookshop had remained closed, and Flora had deliberately avoided all calls other than those from Tanya, Jean, Betty and Sally. She simply couldn't face the village right now.

Word would have spread like wildfire that there had been another murder at The Rise, there would be gossip and speculation, and Flora simply hadn't had the strength to go out and face it.

That would come to an end today, however, when she would brave the Sunday morning church service. Sally had reassured her that they didn't expect her there, but Flora felt obliged to be present when the vicar announced the news of both the wedding and the fete. She didn't want he or Sally to have to deal with the barrage of questions and complaints that she knew would be swiftly incoming as soon as the service ended. It was her responsibility, though not Adam's and Flora had finally managed to persuade him to stay at home, despite the man's protestations that he wanted to accompany her for moral support.

Flora looked at herself in the mirror. Her hair had been washed and blow dried neatly, and she had attempted some make-up before dressing in a sombre chiffon dress of light grey. A pale lemon cardigan completed the outfit, with matching shoes and bag. To the world, she would look the part of lady of the manor, but inside Flora felt like a fraud and a failure. How the villagers wouldn't see right through her disguise she had no idea.

Adam drove her to the church – mainly for safety, but also so that Flora didn't have to endure the whispers and stares of walking to church alongside her neighbours – and she slipped into the chapel quietly through the side entrance.

"Flora lass, I've been waiting for ye, here come and sit with us," Betty shouted across the pew as soon as she saw her, causing all eyes to turn to Flora.

Keeping her head lowered and her eyes cast down, Flora shuffled along the empty row until she was sitting next to her friends.

"What's all this about?" Betty asked gently, hooking an index finger under Flora's chin and lifting her head gently until their eyes met, "Don't you be acting all guilty like. No one thinks you've got anything to be blamed for." She grasped one of Flora's hands between the two of hers and squeezed tight.

"I'm not, I…" Flora felt her eyes begin to fill and quickly blinked back the tears, "It's hard, Betty, it was his brother." Flora hadn't told the older couple any of the details surrounding the death, only that it was Adam's kin who had been killed up at the big house.

"Aye lass, right sad it is. Did he get our card? Harry posted it through the letterbox, that policeman standing duty outside your cottage wouldn't let him knock and hand it to you personally."

"Yes, yes, thank you Betty," Flora was glad that the vicar made his way up the central aisle at that moment, forcing a halt to the conversation. She smoothed her hands over her floaty skirt and focused straight ahead. Even the Marshall girls hadn't turned around to chat to her before the organ struck up the opening chords, no doubt told by Sally to give Flora some space, and for some reason that made her feel even more hollow inside.

To say the service had been uncomfortable was an understatement. The whispers of pity and curiosity when the vicar announced the postponement of the wedding had morphed quickly into louder sighs of disappointment and outright grumbling when he had gone on to talk about the village fete. James had cleverly woven it all into a sermon about everything on God's earth having its season, yet the congregation seemed to be chattering over half of it, and Flora felt the tension in her shoulders and back grow. She didn't once turn around, instead keeping her poise ramrod straight on the uncomfortable wooden bench.

It was in fact Betty who seemed to break first. The moment the sermon was finished and the vicar asked them all to bow their heads for the prayers, the older woman stood abruptly, apologised to the man on the pulpit, and then turned, her eyes blazing.

"Will you pipe down!" she commanded, bringing an

instant hush to the place, "A man has died. A family are grieving, and you have no concern other than for yourselves. Think on it, what if it was one of your blood and bone, eh? Would you want a fancy shmancy wedding or a game of hook a duck? Of course you wouldn't! Check yerselves before ye speak again about it!"

"Ah, very well said Mrs. Bentley," the vicar responded, looking somewhat astounded, while his wife turned from her seat in the pew in front of them and gave Betty a thankful smile. The service proceeded without any further commotion, and Flora was glad when it was finally over. She was so tempted to just slip out of the side door, but was determined not to take the coward's way out. Thanking Betty for her support and promising to visit the couple soon, Flora took a deep breath in and stood to face the villagers.

And... nothing.

Everyone was filing out in the usual manner or standing in small groups chatting quietly. Flora spotted Amy, Gareth and Lewis standing in the centre of an excited group of ladies, all of whom were admiring what must be Amy's new engagement ring. Flora made a mental note to congratulate the couple and to buy Amy some flowers when life returned to normal. Whenever that might be. Edwina Edwards turned to give Flora a disdainful glare, but that was par for the course on any regular Sunday!

Betty's public admonishment seemed to have done the trick, and Flora was happy to see Lily making her way towards her from the back of the church, her jolly face graced by its usual beaming smile, and putting Flora immediately at ease.

"Flora, it's so good to see you," Lily was slightly breathless and her face redder than usual, "we were late so had to sit right at the back... I mean that's usual for us, so I guess I should just say I was in my normal seat," she chuckled to herself, "but had I got here in time I was planning to sit with you. Sally spoke to me yesterday about having an Autumn fayre up at the farm and me and Stan are right up for it! We can have the farm shop open and tractor rides, animal petting, the lot!"

"I'm so relieved, thank you so much Lily."

"Aye, and right sorry we are for your loss too," Lily lowered her voice, "don't you be listenin' to any of those ornery old uns, you just do what you need to," she leant forwards and gave Flora a huge hug before pulling away again.

"Thank you, Lily, you are a true friend," Flora felt overcome by emotion once again and tried hard to hold back the tears.

"Of course," Lily beamed at her, "I haven't seen Tanya about much though. Do you know if she's unwell?"

"Tanya? Oh, ah, yes, she's definitely been under the weather."

"Ah bless her, I'll have to pop round with some of my fiery homemade chutney, put the hairs on anyone's chest that would!"

Flora couldn't help a small laugh, remembering the time she had bought some of the condiment in question for she and Adam to try. It had taken two glasses of milk and a bowl of ice cream to calm the burning in her throat after just a small amount, "Yes, that'll do the trick!"

By the time Lily had rushed off – always dashing everywhere – and Flora looked up, the crowd at the back of the chapel had all but dissipated and she took her time breathing in the peace of the place.

"How is everything, Flora?" the vicar asked, making his way back down the aisle after greeting everyone as they left the church.

"As well as can be expected. Thank you, Reverend, for the announcements, and for all of your kind words the other day."

"Absolutely my pleasure, it's what I'm here for. And how is Adam?"

"Ah, well, quiet."

"To be expected," Flora had briefly filled James and Sally in over the phone the previous day, "let him know I'm always here if he wants to chat."

"I will, thank you," Flora accepted his handshake and then made her way out into the sunshine, where Adam was waiting in the car to make sure she got home safely.

In truth, with Dmitriy still at large, and McArthur having told them that Vik was showing no signs of swapping information on his boss's whereabouts in return for a plea deal, there was no way that her fiancé could even begin to move on. Nor Tanya either, and Flora could only imagine the fear her friend must be living with.

No, something needed to be done, but what? And without bringing more danger to the village and to those she loved.

Flora had no idea what that solution could be.

TWENTY-SIX

That she was hoping for a quiet afternoon made little difference. They had barely eaten the roast dinner that Adam had prepared while Flora was at church when the young officer on duty at the front door knocked to ask if the couple were expecting visitors.

A quick look confirmed that it was Shona and Will, so Adam gave permission for them to be allowed inside. Flora plastered a smile on her face, wished she hadn't changed into leggings and a tee-shirt that were quite so old and scruffy, and went about preparing a pot of Earl Grey as if on autopilot.

"Not the Vet! Not the Vet!" Reggie screeched from his

perch in the lounge as soon as he saw the identity of the visitors, and became so agitated that Flora had to bribe him with grapes to calm the silly bird down.

"Hush," she said on a sigh to the bundle of feathers sitting on her counter top, "he hasn't come here for you!"

"We're so sorry to bother you both," Shona began when they were all assembled in the cosy sitting room, enjoying the homemade banana bread which the pub landlady had kindly brought. It reminded Flora that she needed to cancel the wedding cake... Oh! And the wedding planners, in fact, and also made her nostalgic for the days not so long ago when she was doing her own baking.

"Not at all," Flora replied politely, "what can we do for you?"

"Well, we wanted to strike while the iron's hot, so to speak," Will squeezed his hands together and then rubbed them up and down his thighs as he spoke, "ah, we don't want you to think we're speaking out of turn though, so please just say if our suggestion makes you uncomfortable, or we've crossed a line, made an error of judgement, we haven't had long to think on it, just since we heard the announcement in church this morning..."

"What my fiancé is trying to say," Shona interjected quickly, "is that we were wondering if you've had time to cancel the wedding arrangements? I mean, is everything still booked?"

"Ah, well, actually yes," Flora began in a rather stilted fashion "but I am going to deal with that myself…"

"No! No, we aren't suggesting we do that for you," Shona was quick to clarify, "we were just wondering if we could take the place of the bride and groom, make use of it all so to speak? We would pay you, of course…"

"Well," Flora didn't need more than a moment to think on it. She smiled at Adam and he nodded in reply, "yes, what a wonderful idea! We can work out the money and all that, but my goodness, it'll be just what the village needs!"

"Thank you so much!" Shona's voice rose in excitement, and she clasped Will's hands in hers. The vet himself blushed from his forehead all the way down his neck and under his plaid shirt, not helped by the little green bird who started shrieking "You sexy beast!" on repeat.

"It's our pleasure," Adam spoke for the first time, "Flora did such a grand job of organising the event, I'm so proud of her."

Flora felt his praise down to her toes and was acutely aware of her own face heating, "Let's have something stronger to celebrate, shall we?" she asked as she rushed off to the kitchen to find the celebration glasses and the bottle of prosecco she'd been saving for a special occasion.

No sooner had the bubbly been poured, then there was another polite knock on the front door.

"Excuse me," Adam said, though Flora caught the shadow that passed across his features. Her stomach sank so quickly it felt like she was on a rollercoaster, though her smile didn't falter in front of her guests.

Flora needn't have worried, as her fiancé returned two minutes later followed by Amy and Gareth. Seeing them, Reggie flew down the hallway as if looking for his little buddy Lewis.

"Oh, we left him with his grandparents," Amy spoke to the bird directly as if understanding exactly who he was missing, and then realised suddenly on entering the now rather cramped sitting room that they were not the only visitors. Her face fell for a moment and

Flora caught it, just before her friend smiled around at them all, rubbing her baby bump gently.

"Come in, we were just having a small celebration," Flora tried to put Amy at her ease.

"We can come back," Gareth offered.

"No, no, the more the merrier," Flora gave them both a glass, filling Amy's with apple juice, and then explained the reason for the toast. The longer she spoke, the farther Amy's face fell, until the heavily pregnant woman looked as if she might cry.

"Is everything okay, Amy?" Shona asked gently.

"Ah, yes, well… it's just that you seem to have beaten us to it."

It all became clear for Flora in that second. Gareth had mentioned wanting to be married before the baby came, and they had probably seen this as the perfect opportunity. There was a solution though…

"Well, I can think of…" Flora began, trying to find the most diplomatic path, not wanting to trample on Shona and Will's romantic plans.

"You could share with us!" Shona saved her the worry, "We could have a double wedding! We'd be inviting most of the same crowd anyway, and the manor house is plenty big enough. Half the costs, twice the joy! What do you think?"

Amy looked at Gareth, her eyes full of hope.

"That is a perfect solution," Gareth grinned widely, "if it's okay with Flora and Adam of course?"

"Nothing would give me more joy than sharing in your joint happy day," Flora replied, and meaning it wholeheartedly.

They all needed this. Needed something on the horizon to look forward to, something new and fresh and without any skeletons in closets or shadows in corners.

"I'll phone the Crawfords and explain, and then ask them to contact you. Feel free to change any little details, I'm not precious about any of it."

Flora caught Adam looking at her when she finished speaking, his face a mixture of pride and sadness.

"I love you," he mouthed from across the room, touching his hand to his heart, and Flora felt the weight of his words as if he had spoken them straight into her soul.

Their time would come, she knew it, and when it

did it would be on their own terms.

TWENTY-SEVEN

Flora had been thinking. Well, to be more specific, her mind had been doing that annoying whirring thing that wouldn't allow her to focus properly on anything else. Two weeks had passed since the tragic incident at The Rise and she and Adam were both going stir crazy. Tanya, too, had been in regular contact saying that she was feeling suffocated seeing nothing but the same four walls every day, and that she was taking it out on Pat which wasn't what she wanted at all. Poor Reggie had taken to rummaging in Flora's room and coming out with bright scarves or jewellery – anything to play with and relieve his boredom. If he knew it was something he shouldn't have, then all the better, as a good chase around the house with Flora huffing and puffing behind him was always a great distraction!

Every time Flora broached the subject of things returning to normal, of re-opening the tearoom and getting on with life, Adam responded with the same thing – that Dmitriy would be biding his time for that very thing. For them to let their guards down and think it had all blown over. Then, Adam said, he would strike. Apparently, the team that had been investigating the gang over the longer term now had a mole in place, who had reported back that Dmitriy was fixated on Tanya, furious with her in fact. He believed that if she had given him the information his men needed, then he wouldn't have lost both Carl and Vik. The fact that Carl had turned against him and attempted to pull off a double cross had also enraged the Russian, and he planned to make his former girlfriend pay for what he believed was her part in all of it. Adam, so McArthur relayed, had been punted to second on his hit list. Needless to say, none of this had made its way to Tanya's ears as there was no point in making her more anxious.

It was all of this that had Flora thinking the situation through on what felt like an endless loop, until finally one morning, seeing Reggie with a rather lurid green scarf that had been in the pile for the charity shop, she had the answer. It would take all of her powers of persuasion to convince Adam, she knew, as well as some help from McArthur in reassuring her fiancé that the ruse would work, but Flora was determined to try. Something had to be done, and the police weren't making any headway. They knew Dmitriy's location now but needed to catch him in the act. Not an easy feat when the man normally refused to get his own hands dirty…

The tearoom felt cold and neglected despite the early morning sun shining through the small windows. Flicking on the central heating to give the place a cosy glow, Flora pottered about happily, glad to be back in the familiar setting. She laid out the ingredients she had brought with her on the counter, taking them from her large tote bag one by one and hoping that the trembling in her hands wasn't too noticeable.

"Scones first," she said to Reggie who, having flown three laps of the tearoom and bookshop, was now settled on his perch surveying his kingdom as if he had never left the place, "then maybe some jam tarts and fairy cakes."

"Welcome to the tearoom!" the bird chirped happily, fluffing his feathers in anticipation of all the attention his was used to receiving from customers.

That the only person who had been told about this grand opening was Dmitriy, via the police mole within his organisation, was a fact which Flora was trying hard not to dwell upon. As far as the criminal boss knew, the news had been well-advertised within the village, with a celebratory afternoon tea offered to everyone at four o'clock.

Flora hoped that the last part may be true, just not this day – tomorrow, if her plan was successful. And that was a very big 'if'.

"I'm still not sure love," Adam said for what seemed like the hundredth time that morning, appearing from the bookshop with the weary expression that told her he knew exactly what Flora's response was going to be. The same thing it had been every other time they had discussed how today would go.

"Well, I am… I just hope it isn't all for nothing. I mean, what if he waits another week or two?" Despite Flora's outward determination, inside she was well aware that there were so many ways in which her plan could fail.

"The feedback from inside is that his blood's boiling to the extent the man is lacking patience and good judgement. Meaning he's likely to be hot-headed and react at the first opportunity, but also making the whole thing ten times more dangerous. Really, love, let's speak to Tanya and…"

"No! Thank you, Adam, I understand, but McArthur and that bloke you call Sir…"

"Carruthers."

"Yes, Carruthers, he seemed happy enough with the plan when they came to the coach house, didn't he?"

"He was prepared to humour you, yes."

Flora forced herself to ignore the sting in his words, knowing it came from a place of care and concern, "Well then, let's get this show on the road."

TWENTY-EIGHT

It was well past lunchtime and the sun had moved around to the other side of the old, stone building, when finally there came the familiar tinkle of the bell above the door. A new sense of alert filled the air which, when combined with the familiar noise, caused the little bird on his perch to wake suddenly.

"Get out of it!" He shrieked, before apparently becoming more aware of his surroundings and chirping a very sociable, "Welcome to the tearoom, so cosy!"

"Cosy indeed," the tall man who approached him replied with an accent that was clearly eastern European, holding out a bony finger and tickling Reggie under the chin.

The bird responded with confusion, the vibes he was getting from the strange visitor's nearness at odds with his gentle touch, "Watch Out! Hide it all! She's a cracker! Secrets and Lies! I'm all shook up!" the little bird released a string of his favourite phrases, apparently unsure as to which was the best fit for the situation.

The man gave a small smile, though his lips remained firmly pressed together and his eyes kept their reptilian coldness. His frame was not overly bulky, but it filled out his expensive suit well – an outfit which set him as out of place in this rural backwater. Each movement appeared measured. There was no hurry, no urgency to his actions, as the man turned slowly to face the counter. He trailed his hand over the first table he passed as he made his slow approach, running his fingers over the crocheted doily and then over a china saucer as if committing the different textures to memory.

His eyes never left the back of the woman who was bent over, attending to the tray of cakes which she was taking from the oven. Her short, purple leather skirt rose to an almost indecent level and she pulled it down with not a little irritation, her sparkly pink, acrylic nails catching on the material. As if she hadn't heard the doorbell, or the interaction with the bird, she took off her oven gloves and began dispensing her creations onto the cooling tray, pausing mid-action to brush her peroxide blond hair back from her face.

"Tatiana," the one word, said in such a commanding tone, nearly brought her to her knees, her legs already like jelly. She forced herself to stand her ground, and acted as if she had not heard him, "Tatiana! You must've known I was coming for you!" The second time he said the woman's name it was spat out with considerably more anger and venom, as if the speaker's hold on his own composure was a tenuous one.

Still she ignored him, which seemed to tip the man over the edge, snapping the last thread of his patience. Where the casual walk from the parrot's perch had taken him what felt like minutes, he was around the obstacle of the counter and standing right behind her in the briefest of seconds. The woman felt the hairs on the back of her neck stand on end, and then the heat of his breath as the man came far too close for comfort.

"Tatiana," he pronounced each of the four syllables slowly, imbuing each with the anger that was barely held in check. She could feel his whole body buzzing from it, yet still she made no move to reply, "Tatiana, look at me when you take your last breath!"

She spun then, saw the shock in his eyes that she was not the woman he had taken her to be, and took advantage of his moment of hesitation to dart to the side. In the same instant, the sound of a gun cocking replaced the heavy silence, and the man felt the metal as it touched his temple...

"I'm still shaking," Flora whispered, clutching her cup of sweet tea with both hands and wishing she had thought to bring her own clothes to change back into. At least she'd been able to take off the itchy wig.

"I know love, I know, you did so well."

"I'm surprised Carruthers' back hadn't seized up from hiding under the counter for so long. I'll have to put all my pots and pans back in that space..." Flora found she was waffling, the delayed shock only now settling in.

"There's time for all that tomorrow. Why don't we go back to the coach house and..." Adam was interrupted by the door bursting open and Tanya rushing in like a ball of energy that had been kept contained for far too long.

"Flora! McArthur has been to see us. My goodness

Flora, you silly woman, what were you thinking?"

"Silly old bird," Reggie agreed, bobbing up on down on his perch and angling for Tanya's attention.

"Hush you," Tanya stroked his feathers before plonking herself down on the chair next to Flora in dramatic fashion, "it seems you are a match for me with your acting skills, my friend, but I wish you had shared your plan. I would never have let you take my place."

"And that's exactly why I didn't tell you," Flora replied, squeezing Tanya's hand, "it was my idea, my choice to make. And I was very safe, really, we seemed to have a whole unit of police here, in the bookshop and even in the tiny bathroom!"

They both knew that her safety hadn't been guaranteed at all, not with such a ruthless man, but Tanya seemed happy to let the subject drop, "Well, I will always be grateful to you, thank you." She turned away to hide the tears which had sprung up, and Adam excused himself under the pretence of fetching her a cup of tea.

Pat, who had followed his wife into the tearoom, and had thus far hovered uncomfortably just inside the doorway, came forward then and put his arm around Tanya's shoulders, "I can't tell you the relief, I…" his voice cracked and the policeman murmured something about helping Adam with the drinks.

"So," Tanya said when the women were alone, "I hear we are to have two weddings. But neither of them are yours? Are you sure, Flora?"

"I am. It's not the right time for us. We want something quiet, something private and personal and for that we can't get married in the village. Besides, Adam is still grieving and they have given him extended leave from work. He's thinking of taking a trip up to the highlands to do some hiking and clear his mind. Which leaves our honeymoon that's already booked and paid for in Yorkshire, and we were wondering if you would like to come with me? I know you could do with the break as much as me, and I thought we could invite Betty and Jean too? I'll rearrange the booking at the hotel and change the bridal suite to two twin rooms."

"Really? Oh my goodness, Flora, I haven't had a holiday since I moved up here! I've never been to Yorkshire. Are you sure? I will pay my way of course," Tanya was like an excited child on Christmas Eve and it made Flora's heart happy to be able to bring her friend such joy after the harrowing time they had endured.

"Absolutely! It's settled then."

"But what about the tearoom?"

"You leave that to me, I..." Flora didn't get to finish her sentence as the door to the tearoom flew open, the bell jangling erratically.

"You were right, Hilda! She is open!" Betty rushed into the room, still looking behind her as she spoke to whom Flora presumed was Hilda May.

"News travels fast," Tanya observed drily.

"It's like living in a goldfish bowl," Flora whispered and both women laughed, the newfound feeling of lightness and relief really quite blissful.

TWENTY-NINE

The double wedding of the decade was taking place in just two days' time, and since one of the brides was expecting and the other worked with alcohol all day long, they had opted to have a hens' tea party instead of the usual hen do. It never ceased to amaze Flora what the women of the village could conjure up on a moment's notice, from perfectly decorated, wedding-themed biscuits, to miniature fruit cakes, iced to look like wedding cakes. (Courtesy of Betty, who finally managed to make the cake she wanted, albeit in miniature form!) The atmosphere was one of community and celebration, and Flora soaked it all in. Now that it wasn't her own nuptials, the pressure had been lifted and she intended to enjoy every minute of the coming days.

"Can you hold that end while I get this on straight?" Rosa asked, as she attached the delicately-crocheted bunting in the shape of bells above the windows in the tearoom.

"It's so beautiful, Rosa," Amy observed from where she sat on a chair at the table next to them, her feet up on another seat, "can I book you to make some things for my little one?"

"I may have already started," Rosa blushed and the women laughed.

Reggie flew from table to table, inspecting the arrangements and then, when happy that all was to his satisfaction, he came to land on Amy's shoulder. Earlier, he had tried to perch himself on her protruding bump, but Flora had shooed him off, much to the little bird's chagrin.

"Everyone will be arriving in half an hour, shall I take him home?" Flora asked the younger woman, concerned that the excitable parrot would pester her for the whole afternoon.

"No, no, let him stay," Amy smiled, "I think he can just sense the baby. Besides, once everyone's here he'll be spoilt for choice with people to fuss over him and to feed him titbits!"

"Oh, I'm sure he will," Flora said, rather more sardonically, eying her little friend who had fluffed out his chest and was currently cleaning his wing feathers – must look his best for his adoring fans!

There were enough pots of tea drunk that afternoon to sink a ship, dozens of cakes of all shapes and sizes, and all with the common theme of the upcoming wedding. Toasts had been raised to the brides, and to Flora for the sacrifice they all felt she had made – though Flora herself didn't see it that way at all. In all honesty, letting Amy and Shona have their big day on what was meant to be hers had been liberating.

Thankfully Reggie had, for the most part, managed to button his beak. His only memorable outburst had been when Tanya had brought out the cream scones – halved, smothered in Cornish clotted cream, and each adorned with three, juicy ripe strawberries from the farm, the little bird's eyes had been out on stalks at the sight.

At first, he had flown to Tanya's shoulder and tried to butter her up, with "She's a corker!" and "You sexy beast!" Though Flora did wonder if he was referring more to the fruity treat than to the woman carrying the tray! When this had only served to get him a quick,

"Desist silly bird!" Reggie flew over to Flora, as if telling tales.

Squawks of "Old trout!" and "Bad bird!" were levelled in Tanya's direction until Jean either took pity on him, or simply couldn't bear the noise any longer, and gave the naughty parrot one of the strawberries from her own plate.

"She's a cracker!" Reggie bobbed up and down happily, clearly thoroughly pleased with himself and his victory.

Flora had noted with relief that Tanya seemed to be much more like her old self. Her outfit was back to being her own quirky, rather flamboyant taste, and she had thrown herself into helping with the event with gusto. Of course, Flora knew as well as anybody that what was presented on the outside was often very different to what was hidden beneath, and she resolved to give her friend all the support she needed to move on from recent events. Hopefully, their holiday in Yorkshire would give plenty of opportunity for that, and they would be able to help each other heal.

With all of the women pitching in to clear the tables and to wash the dishes, tidying up from the lovely get together took almost no time at all, and Flora was once

again deeply grateful for the community she had
found in Baker's Rise.

"All done, love? Was it everything the brides wanted?"
Adam asked as he collected her from the tearoom at
the end of the day.

"Yes, it was... perfect, actually," Flora let out a happy
sigh, shooing Reggie out of the door ahead of her so
that she could lock up.

"Aw, I'm glad. You all deserved a relaxing afternoon,
that's for sure. Now, are you positive you're ready for
this?"

"I am if you are. I mean, we have to be up there to
celebrate the weddings the day after tomorrow, that'll
be a bit difficult if neither of us can bear to step foot in
the place," her words sounded certain, though the
quietness of her response betrayed Flora's inner
anxiety at the prospect. The issue of the manor house
had loomed large in her life both physically and
metaphorically for far too long.

"Onwards and upwards then," Adam said, not just
referring to the hill in front of them.

"Yes, let's just do it. I know it was a cop out me giving

the Crawfords the key and letting them get on with it once the crime scene cleaners had finished in the kitchen, but I just couldn't face it. Any of it."

"Aye lass, I know, I should've stepped up and…"

"No! That wasn't what I meant, you have more reason than I do to not want to ever go in there again. I'm so sorry, Adam."

"What are you sorry for?" He stopped in the middle of the gravel driveway and turned to face her fully, "None of it, do you hear me? None was your fault. We'll start again, when we've both had our trips away, we'll reassess where we are and what we want, and that old house will be a part of that discussion."

He kissed her gently on the lips, but Flora needed more. More reassurance, more of him. She stood on her tiptoes and pressed herself closer, deepening their kiss. When Adam responded, cupping the back of her neck and returning the force of her affection, Flora felt like she had come home. Here, in this man's arms. This was home. Not a building or a place. Just wherever he was.

THIRTY

The flower arrangements were in place, the folk band
had set up in the new drawing-come-function room,
the caterers were busy in the kitchen and marquee, and
Flora stood at the front door of The Rise, ready to
welcome the guests who were walking up from the
church. She and Adam had rushed back up in the car
as soon as the service was finished, to make sure
everything was on track while the two newlywedded
couples were having photos taken on the village
Green.

"You look beautiful," Adam whispered in her ear,
making Flora blush the same shade of pink as her
fancy hat.

"So do you," she replied, turning to kiss him on the cheek.

"No regrets?" he asked, the uncertainty in his voice endearing.

"None at all. This wasn't right for us." Flora had no doubts whatsoever.

"I love you," Adam smiled, the tension in his shoulders relaxing.

"And I love you, with all my heart, and I can't wait to be your wife."

Will Flora and Adam manage to tie the knot on their own terms? And, more importantly, will she survive a holiday with three of her close friends, on what was meant to be her honeymoon?

*Join Flora and Reggie in, "**A Walk in the Parkin**," the seventh instalment in the Baker's Rise Mysteries series.*

R. A. Hutchins

A Walk In The Parkin

Baker's Rise Mysteries Book Seven

Publication Date September 30th 2022

The residents of Baker's Rise are on tour in this seventh story in the series. Of course, the book is jam packed with the usual cosy humour and unexpected happenings which make these mysteries so popular!

A honeymoon in Yorkshire was just what Flora needed – it's a shame that nothing regarding the trip has gone to plan. If three's a crowd, then what's four?

With a feathery stowaway in her luggage and a mix-up with rooms, it's fair to say that the holiday doesn't start well!

Flora tries to make the best of it, but when a lifeless body turns up at the hotel's baking class, it's not only romance that's dead!

Packed with twists and turns, colourful characters and a distinct lack of romance for once, this new mystery will certainly leave you hungry for more!

R. A. Hutchins

Fresh as a Daisy

The Lillymouth Mysteries Book One

Coming early 2023!

Keep your eyes peeled for a brand new series coming to Amazon later this year!

Featuring a new lady vicar, a grumpy vicarage cat, and a seaside town in Yorkshire full of hidden secrets and more than a mystery or two!

R. A. Hutchins

ABOUT THE AUTHOR

Rachel Hutchins lives in northeast England with her husband, three children and their dog Boudicca. She loves writing both mysteries and romances, and enjoys reading these genres too! Her favourite place is walking along the local coastline, with a coffee and some cake!

You can connect with Rachel and sign up to her monthly **newsletter** via her website at: www.authorrachelhutchins.com

Alternatively, she has social media pages on:

Facebook: www.facebook.com/rahutchinsauthor

Instagram: www.instagram.com/ra_hutchins_author

R. A. Hutchins

OTHER BOOKS BY R. A. HUTCHINS

"The Angel and the Wolf"

What do a beautiful recluse, a well-trained husky, and a middle-aged biker have in common?
Find out in this poignant story of love and hope!

When Isaac meets the Angel and her Wolf, he's unsure whether he's in Hell or Heaven.
Worse still, he can't remember taking that final step.
They say that calm follows the storm, but will that be the case for Isaac?

Fate has led him to her door,
Will she have the courage to let him in?

"To Catch A Feather" (Found in Fife Book One)

When tragedy strikes an already vulnerable Kate Winters, she retreats into herself, broken and beaten. Existing rather than living, she makes a journey North to try to find herself, or maybe just looking for some sort of closure.

Cameron McAllister has known his own share of grief and love lost. His son, Josh, is now his only priority. In his forties and running a small coffee shop in a tiny Scottish fishing village, Cal knows he is unlikely to find love again.

When the two meet and sparks fly, can they overcome their past losses and move on towards a shared future, or are the memories which haunt them still too real?

These books, as well as others by Rachel, can be found on Amazon worldwide in e-book and paperback formats, as well as free to read on Kindle Unlimited.

Printed in Great Britain
by Amazon